No One Dies in Branson

ALSO BY KATHRYN BUCKSTAFF
Branson and Beyond

No One Dies *in* B·R·A·N·S·O·N

Kathryn Buckstaff

ST. MARTIN'S PRESS ★ NEW YORK

This is a work of fiction. Any similarity to actual inci-
dents and any resemblance to persons living or dead
is purely coincidental.

Design by Sara Stemen

LIBRARY OF CONGRESS CATALOGING-IN-PUBLICATION DATA

Buckstaff, Kathryn.
    No one dies in Branson / Kathryn Buckstaff.
      p. cm.
    "A Thomas Dunne book."
    ISBN 0-312-11036-7
    1. Branson (Mo.)—Fiction. 2. Country
music—Missouri—Branson—Fiction. I. Title.
PS3552.U3453N6   1994
813'.54—dc20   94-602
                                          CIP

First Edition: August 1994
10 9 8 7 6 5 4 3 2 1

*This book is dedicated
to my sons,
Brett and Brian,
my parents and many friends,
whose love and encouragement
have enabled me to dream big*

Age appears to be best in four things—
old wood best to burn, old wine to
drink, old friends to trust, and
old authors to read.
—*FRANCIS BACON*

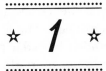

The dead silence in the cabin frightened Emily, and she flicked on the television, where Vanna White was turning letters. Emily slung her suitcase onto the bed and looked out at Table Rock Lake, as still as steel in the darkness beyond the front windows. She turned on both table lamps and closed the drapes. No matter how often she traveled, she always felt a little edgy the first night in a new motel, but this time it was worse. "Welcome to the Ozarks, girl," she said to herself.

Emily laid her white blazer on the bed, slipped off her heels, and pushed back her thick shoulder-length hair. For a moment she thought of the few gray strands she'd eliminated that morning. At thirty-eight, she wasn't about to give in to the salt-and-pepper look or the shorter haircuts popular with her working-women colleagues. Beneath her sleek Buscati business suits lurked a rebellious heart.

She reached into the small Styrofoam cooler she'd bought and popped the top of a Milwaukee Best Light. The thought of a cigarette entered her mind and then she thought of her forty-six days of abstinence and sighed. "Just don't think about it," she admonished herself, not for the first time.

She undid the latches on her Samsonite case and

searched at the side for her loafers. She'd stroll down to the lakeshore. It might be relaxing to see it in the light of the half-moon. She had tried to think positively about this trip since her editor at the *Tampa Tribune* had given her the assignment a month ago. The idea of staying in a secluded resort surrounded by cedar trees had seemed appealing then. Nights in her ninth-floor Tampa apartment were filled with the blare of horns, sirens, doors slamming down the hall. But the closer she'd got to the Bitterroot Resort, the more uneasy she had felt. "Old ghosts," she had muttered behind the wheel of the rented black Ford Probe. "Get a grip on yourself, girl." She had accelerated and tried to enjoy the car's power that was pushing her along the winding road, straight into Branson, Missouri.

Emily opened the cabin's door. It was a warm, slightly humid July evening, but the air smelled like Christmas trees. Nearby, dry leaves rustled. Emily shut the door partway and turned on the yellow porch light. Peering through the opening, she saw a shape move beneath a bush. A dark, fluffy tail emerged, then glowing eyes turned her way. Emily closed the door and turned the dead bolt. A bath, a beer, and a book will do, she thought. Leave the night to the critters. From somewhere in the cabin, she caught a sweet scent and her memory connected it with a smell she'd nearly forgotten. It was like a whiff of Southern Comfort from the pint her daddy had always carried in his overalls.

When she was five, she had thought he was the biggest man in the world. She recalled a day when he'd taken her fishing. He'd held her little hand as they walked across the pasture to the pond, where a wooden rowboat rested. He had picked her up to put her into the boat, and she'd hugged his neck, not minding the scratch of his two days' growth of beard against her cheek. He had kissed her, and she'd smelled the sweetness of his breath. His curly hair was graying around the edges, and if Emily had been older, she might have seen how much his meaty features resembled Babe Ruth's.

When she was seated in the boat, her father had handed her a short fishing pole, put his own longer version into the boat, and pushed them offshore. It was just a neighbor's farm pond, stocked each spring with new bass fingerlings to keep up the supply, but for Emily being on this lake with her father was special. Her mother never went with them. The sun was just coming over the hill behind the pond, and Emily shivered a little in the morning chill. Even in summer, it often got cool at night in the Ozark hills.

Her father took a slightly rusted Prince Albert tobacco can from the pocket of his overalls and dumped part of the contents into his hand. A fat earthworm squirmed its way out of the dirt. He wrapped the worm around the hook on Emily's pole, sticking the worm twice, and then tossed the line into the pond. After he'd baited his own hook and propped the pole between his knees, he pulled out a new Prince Albert can and paper, and rolled himself a cigarette, then lit it with a wooden match from another pocket. Next he pulled out the flat pint bottle and took a swig from it. He smiled at Emily as she bobbed her fishing line in the water to tempt the fish, just as he had taught her. "Baby girl," her father had said, smiling at her, "there's no one as lucky as us today."

Emily turned on the bathroom light. The room was as well appointed as the rest of the log cabin. A wicker basket filled with pink towels sat on a small table beside the bronze-doored shower, an enameled dish held colored soap balls, and above the shining Jacuzzi tub, a glass-eyed stuffed pheasant, ready for flight, gazed impassively at her. A hunting lodge. How appropriate for a journalist, she thought.

She began unpacking her suitcase and hanging clothes in the cedar-lined closet. She took off her navy silk blouse and pin-striped slacks, peeled off the panty hose, and unfastened her black lace bra. She kneaded her small breasts for a moment, then stretched out her arms, arching her back and rolling her head from side to side. The plane ride from Tampa through Dallas then St. Louis and finally to Springfield, Missouri, had been bad enough. Airplane seats certainly weren't designed for Emily's petite, five-feet-two-inch frame. Then there was the hour-long drive south to Branson. By the time she'd found the resort, the car was a mess. An empty Coke can mingled with a Snickers wrapper, and dried wormlets of Taco Bell cheese and lettuce laced the floor mats. Still, no cigarette butts in the ashtray.

She tossed her peach cotton robe on the bed. From the suitcase she took the worn volume of Robert Browning's poetry and laid it on the nightstand. Her mother had loved that book too, although she could barely read and had no idea what Browning's poetry meant. On the rare occasions Emily came home from college to the meager trailer house near Jacksonville, her mother would touch the book shyly, in the same reverent way she handled the family Bible. "You'll be as handy as the pocket on a shirt when you get through that college."

From the time she was in her teens, Emily had come to hate the sound of her mother's nasal twang and country sayings. She remembered leaning in the doorway of the trailer's small kitchen and watching her mother rummaging in a low cupboard. Her mother wore a drab print housedress she'd bought at a yard sale in the trailer park, stretched taut over her ample backside. "I'm going to bowl these peas that Miz Johnson gave me from her garden this morning," her mother said. "You want to wash them for me?"

"You 'boil' peas, Mother," Emily said, irritated as usual. "It's not 'bowled.' Why don't you stop talking like a hillbilly? This *is* Florida, or did you forget?"

Her mother stood up and turned toward her fifteen-year-old daughter. She held a dented kettle and a cigarette dangled from her mouth. It stuck to her lip for a second when she pulled it away. "We're both hillbillies, Emily. It's the folks down here can't talk right." She hated her mother's grating cackle of a laugh, too. Emily turned and went to her room and shut the door. She gazed with love and sorrow at the photo of her father on her nightstand.

In the 1950s, when a man was having trouble breathing, doctors recommended warmer climates. They didn't know much about emphysema or inhalation therapy or cigarettes. So when Emily was six, her daddy had sold the little hardware store in Blue Eye, Missouri, and moved his wife and daughter south.

Emily had not wanted to go and was an unhappy girl as she tried to make new friends at school. But her clothes were wrong, homemade and dowdy compared to the brightly colored shorts and matching blouses her classmates wore. They made fun of her accent and teased her about how it felt to wear shoes, assuming that she had only run barefoot in the Ozarks. Embarrassed by her country heritage, Emily learned to keep her distance, to pretend she didn't care when she was always the last one chosen for a team. At first, it was a relief to get home every day. Her father was always waiting for her with a hug. He'd sit with her in the evening and watch her practice her penmanship. And when she began to read, he'd listen to the childish stories in her reading books as though they were the most absorbing tales he'd ever heard. That safe place beside him seemed to be all Emily would ever need.

But the warmer climate didn't cure her father's ravaged lungs. During the warm weekend days, her father would sit on the sandy porch and talk about his plans to take her deep-sea fishing. With a gleam in his eye, he'd tell her about swordfish and marlin. While he talked, he'd roll Prince Albert cigarettes and sip Southern Comfort from his pint. At night, she'd fall asleep to the rhythm of his rasping breathing. She was ten when he died.

At eighteen, Emily had left with no regrets for college in Tampa. She worked and took out student loans, and life was meager but civilized in her small apartment. After she began as a junior reporter at the *Tribune,* she sometimes sent a check to her mother to supplement the Social Security, knowing it would probably go for yard-sale junk.

She never took a boyfriend home to meet her mother—until she met Jim. He'd come from a big, happy family, and after they had been dating for nearly a year, he suggested that a trip to Disney World could be coupled with a visit to her mom. "I'd just like to meet her," Jim had said. "I'm not suggesting you take up being barefoot and pregnant or anything, you know?" he cajoled. So they went to Jacksonville.

Her mother had pulled out all the stops to fix a special dinner complete with collard greens. At seventy-two, her mother had hair that was a yellowed gray, trimmed by her own hand in a stubby bob. "I think her country ways are cute," Jim had said on the drive back. "They're not my ways," Emily had replied, staring out the window at the ocean waves. Now at thirty-eight, she was the age her mother had been when she'd had Emily. And she was back in the Ozarks, twenty miles from Blue Eye and the farm pond she had shared with her father.

She took Jim's picture out of the suitcase and looked at the thick, wavy hair and at his broad shoulders where her head rested so comfortably. She could pick up the phone and call him, tell him she was lonely and nervous. But she stopped herself the way she did at holidays when she shopped for greeting cards. She never picked the ones that said "Darling, I'll love you forever." Instead, she bought cards with a noncommittal message from Garfield or Snoopy. Jim never complained even though he did buy the "darling" cards for some occasions. Often he showed his feelings in practical ways—like giving her the gun and a gift certificate to a shooting range.

From the suitcase pocket, she took out the .38 caliber revolver. Now, it felt like cool security in her palm, but she hadn't been thrilled last Christmas morning when she'd opened the gift. "I just want you to be safe, baby," he'd said. Then he'd held out another present. It was the lavender silk teddy she'd admired in the window of Victoria's Secret weeks before when they'd been shopping at the mall. Whenever she thought she'd found a good reason to be irritated with his calm, sensible manner, he'd throw in some sweet, sensitive touch she couldn't resist.

With a sigh of resolve, she slipped Jim's photo back in the suitcase, laid the pistol on the nightstand, and unpacked the neatly labeled folders of notes she'd made on Branson. She arranged the folders on the kitchen table with several reporters' notebooks and a new box of pens. She had thought being a travel writer at the *Tribune* would assure her safe distance from backwoods regions. But the new editor was a country-music fan, and Branson was the capital for country music. The editor had even subscribed to the local Branson newspaper so he could keep up on the latest events there. "Karma strikes again," Emily said as she filled the tub and watched the silent pheasant.

Next Friday's Hot Country awards show would be broadcast nationwide live from Branson. Motel rooms were filling fast with visitors drawn here to see the stars who would be performing. It was a phenomenon, this southwest Missouri town of 3,700. In the past five years, one country artist after another, tired of tours and county-fair circuits, had settled in Branson. Now there were thirty-five theaters where favorites like BoxCar Willie, Mel Tillis, Mickey Gilley, and Roy Clark drew six million visitors a year and raked in big bucks, unshared by agents, managers, or road crews.

Emily slid into the bubbling water. She decided to wear her white sundress and beige blazer to the Hacketts' party tomorrow. The pleasant-sounding chamber of commerce director had suggested in a telephone interview two weeks earlier that the party would be a good way to start her introduction to Branson and that he would arrange the invitation. He had assured her, without much conviction in his voice, that the press was certainly welcome in Branson, but Emily knew better than to take that for granted.

The press was welcome when it served someone's need for publicity, but she had found over the years that if she was pleasant and forthcoming about what she planned to write, she could gain people's trust and write more accurate stories. She had never wanted to be the kind of reporter who looks for juicy stories out of self-interest, in order to win some kind of award. As a travel writer, she didn't have to be concerned with anything sensational except the scenery.

Emily sank into the tub, leaned back, and thought about tomorrow's party. Although she'd been to plenty of posh parties, she couldn't imagine this one. "Belly up to these here collards, folks," she mocked. "Have you tried this catfish stew?" I will not go home with an accent, she told herself.

The water relaxed Emily. She sipped the beer and thought about the candlelit Jacuzzi baths she'd shared with Jim. In the swirling water, Jim would often bring up the subject of their future. For Emily, there was never a good time to talk about marriage. She didn't want to have to work at a relationship, maybe make mistakes, foul it up, and risk unendurable pain. She didn't want to be responsible for a husband's life and well-being, either. She would want him never to die, for one thing, but that was an impossibility, so a relationship could only end in sorrow. She couldn't be with him every moment to make sure he didn't have an auto accident or step in front of a bus on the way to his office. Nor could she make him live his life in a cocoon, even though she was afraid that's exactly what she'd want to do. She had never understood why her mother hadn't taken better care of her father. She could have stopped smoking and made him stop, too, Emily had thought more than once. Emily had learned, after several weeks of counseling to help her break her nicotine addiction, that she still grieved for her father. And she knew, too, that most of the resentment toward her mother was a way of placing the blame for his demise on someone else. After all, she couldn't hate her departed father. She had loved him too much. Her mother, on the other hand, was alive and well, bearing the brunt of Emily's anger. With this knowledge, Emily should have been able to reconcile her differences with her mother, but often she liked to take the easy way out. Maybe it was best to let sleeping dogs lie.

While these fears restricted her relationship with Jim, there were other considerations, too. Time restrictions, for one. After sleeping, eating, and working, Emily was left with about six hours a day to herself and, truth be told, sometimes she didn't want to share that time with anyone. Another fear was that a union with Jim would inevitably lead to suppression of her talents for dealing with people and for writing, the very things that elated Emily nearly every day. She wasn't good at spelling out her fears, at opening up that way, so when the subject came up, Emily often tried to steer the conversation to some innocuous subject. The last time that had happened, only a week ago, it had led to an argument. But Emily didn't like to argue either and had withdrawn. Jim hadn't called all week and Emily wondered if he was punishing her. When she had called to tell him she was leaving for Branson the next day, she thought he sounded hurt when she refused his offer of a ride to the airport. She had assured him there was no need for him to get up that early to see her off, and that she would see him when she returned in a week. But on the plane ride, Emily had wondered if it might not be best just to let the relationship taper off. They had been dating for nearly five years. In that time, Jim had established a successful architecture firm and was settled into a comfortable pattern of life. She didn't know how long he might wait for her to be ready for marriage and a family.

Sometimes Emily felt sure that she wasn't the woman he needed. She had come close more than once to telling him so. But then she would think about the nights that he didn't stay at her apartment when she would wake from a bad dream. In those seconds before reality returned, she would reach to her side for him, to touch his body and feel safe, and she would remember the pang, the clawing in her stomach, when she realized she was alone. She wondered if those empty-bed pangs were the reason single people die younger than married couples. Was it time yet to envision the possibility of growing old alone? Emily wasn't ready to think about that, either. It was like the game her father used to play with her. "Which would you rather be able to do, Emily," he'd asked as they sat in the boat on the quiet pond, "fly or be invisible?" When she was little, Emily had always chosen flying as she watched hawks circling in the cloudless sky. But after they moved to Florida, and school became a daily torture, Emily had thought invisibility was the best choice. When Jim brought up the subject of marriage, Emily often wished both to be invisible and to fly. She had asked Jim the game's question once while they were driving home from work. His practical answer was immediate.

"Fly," he had said. "That way we wouldn't be stuck in all this traffic."

Sharing a duplex with Jim was her best idea, one she hadn't yet suggested to him. It just wasn't so easy to fall in love anymore, she thought.

Switching off the whirlpool jets, Emily stood and reached for a towel. The explosion of metal hitting concrete rang like a gunshot outside the bathroom window, and Emily sprang into the bedroom with her heart pounding. She snatched her robe from the bed, clutching it against her wet body, and reached for the gun. She hit the mute button on the television's remote control and silence returned to the cabin.

Emily glanced toward the door, the curtained front window, then saw herself in the bureau mirror. Naked. Crouching. Holding a pistol. She suddenly felt ridiculous. God, get a grip, she thought. These people don't even lock their doors. You're in the woods, girl. Land of snakes and bugs and things that eat from garbage cans. Coon County, U.S.A.

She laid the pistol back on the nightstand and went to get the towel, eager to be dry and clothed. Emily Stone liked to be prepared for anything. At home, she made sure chairs were pushed in and that no shoes or ironing boards or other obstacles were present that might impede a late-night exit in case of fire. She hated stupid, brainless movie heroines who crept down dark basement stairs or opened locked attic doors. But she was still naked when she heard a woman's angry high-pitched voice outside the cabin.

"The hell with you, you creep. I don't need this shit."

A car door slammed. She heard a motor start, then tires scatter gravel as the car raced away.

Nice little redneck spat, she thought. The loud knock on her door startled her.

"Just a minute," she called out. She put on her robe, wrapping it double across the front, and laid the towel over the gun on the nightstand. "Who is it?"

"I'm your next-door neighbor, ma'am. I just wanted to say hello," said a deep male drawl.

The door had no peephole. No chain. "This isn't Tampa," she reminded herself and slipped the dead bolt.

The man standing in the yellow light was attractive— maybe in his early thirties, with a Billy Ray Cyrus haircut and neatly trimmed beard. He wore a plain black T-shirt and jeans and held up two uncapped bottles of beer.

"I saw you get in earlier, and I just wanted to welcome you to Shangri-La," he said. "My name's Robert Simmons. Can I buy you a beer?"

"Well, thank you," Emily said, smiling politely, "but I'm kind of worn out tonight." She kept hold of the door-knob.

"Where you from?" he persisted.

"Florida," she said. "Tampa."

"Is that right? I lived in St. Petersburg for a while, had a little construction company there, but I'm up from Texas now. Excuse me for being personal, but you look too young to be a Branson tourist."

She found his smile appealing, disarming. "Well, I've heard it takes all kinds here." She returned his drawl so easily. "I appreciate the offer," she said, regaining unac-cented speech and composure, "but I was about ready to turn in. Thanks anyway." She started closing the door.

"Well, that's all right," he went on. "I bet I can drink them both. Did you hear that little disturbance out here just now?"

"Yes, I did," Emily said. Her natural curiosity aroused, she asked, "Friend of yours?"

"Not me," he said, holding out his beer-bottle-filled hands in innocence. "Must have come from the cabin behind us. Did you get a load of the car she was driving?"

"No, I didn't look outside," Emily said. "What kind was it?"

"I don't know," he said. "Just had that low and fast sound. I thought maybe you'd seen what it was."

"No, I didn't," Emily said again. There was an awkward silence. Finally, he shifted his gaze and looked off toward the lake.

"Well, hope you enjoy your visit. Maybe I'll see you again. Good night now." He turned and stepped away into the darkness. Emily relocked the door.

Blowing out her breath through pursed lips, she turned up the television's sound. It was just after nine, and she was worn out. She slipped off her robe and pulled on one of Jim's soft old T-shirts and got into bed. She ate the mint that had been on the pillow and turned to the bookmark in Harold Bell Wright's *The Shepherd of the Hills*, the book that first brought tourists to Branson in the early 1900s. For a while she read about Sammy Lane, the rugged country girl who falls in love with Young Matt. It was an absorbing story and Emily could understand why visitors flocked to the Ozarks to see the scenery and meet the people whose way of life was described in its pages. When she finally fell asleep, the lights in the cabin were still on. Through the night, the television static hissed. Outside, it was quiet.

★ 2 ★

The moment she entered the marble-floored foyer of the Hacketts' house, a smell hit her—like when you're paging through a magazine when someone has opened all the perfume samples. Inside, a young, clean-cut-looking man was seated behind a small cloth-covered table. She told him her name, and he handed her a name tag and welcomed her to the party. "Just go on in and make yourself at home," he said. The tag read Hello. I'm Emily Stone, *Tampa Tribune.* She hated labels. For a journalist it was like wearing a sign that said "Be careful not to say anything significant to me because it could end up in print." But she glanced around the room and saw several others wearing tags, and the young man at the table was still smiling at her expectantly, so she stepped to one side of the entryway to pin on the tag.

She ran her fingers through her hair, and looked up to see a figure who needed no name tag. Kenny Rogers, glistening in a lavender silk suit, walked down the wide staircase. Before she'd quite thought of what she'd say to him, a woman with a mane of stiff blond hair clacked past, balancing on red five-inch spikes.

"Well, baby, if you don't get around, you handsome devil," the blonde cooed to Kenny. Taking his arm, she led him toward a group of people holding wine glasses. It's true what they say about Branson women, Emily thought. Big breasts, big hair.

"Hello, darlin'," a raspy voice sounded behind her. "Come on in. Want some champagne?"

She jumped. She hadn't seen the man approach. The first thing she thought was that he looked like a bad ad for Guess. He wore loose-fitting stonewashed jeans with a denim shirt unbuttoned halfway down the front to reveal a pale, hairless chest and several bright gold chains. His brassy belt buckle, tilted at an angle by his slight potbelly, looked as if it had been borrowed from an old Elvis costume. The man was slim, stood about five ten, and had slick, jet-black hair styled in a 1950s pompadour. She thought he was approaching sixty, but his face had a tightness to it, perhaps the result of a bargain-basement facelift. She recognized the smell of too much English Leather, and remembered pouring Jim's bottle down the drain after she had bought him a bottle of Canoe.

"I'm John Hackett, your host with the most," the man rasped. "And you're our visiting gossip columnist, right?"

"Well, no, I'm not a columnist, Mr. Hackett," Emily said, taking a step backward. She hated people that stood too close. "This is a beautiful home," she said casually. "I've heard so much about it."

"Don't believe everything you read," he said. When he laughed at his own little joke, Emily thought his yellow-stained teeth looked slightly mossy. He stuck a cigarette between them. "You can smoke in this house," he told her with a grin, again leaning close enough so she could smell years of nicotine through the cologne. Emily noticed the man's strange eyes. One pupil was a pinpoint in the sunny entryway. The other pupil gaped, a black hole nearly swallowing up the brown iris. The Cyclops of the Hills, she thought, and suppressed the shiver that rolled up her spine.

John Hackett propelled Emily by the elbow into the

expansive living room. She recognized Moe Bandy, who gave her a polite nod as she passed him. Nearby, she saw John Davidson, familiar to her from *Hollywood Squares* reruns, talking to a petite, attractive woman she recognized as Janet Dailey, the famous romance novelist who had moved to Branson. And standing near the tall windows that looked over the pool and tennis court below, was a small woman, frail and paper-thin. My God, she thought, I'm having cocktails with the Coal Miner's Daughter.

Hackett introduced her to several people in the burgundy-carpeted living room—always with a little laugh as he continued to call her the visiting gossip columnist. After several minutes of polite explanations about the travel article she was there to write, Emily excused herself and wandered onto the terrace. Flat river rocks edged with beds of marigolds led to the tree-shaded swimming pool where a few children splashed and batted around a volleyball. Partway up the hill beside the house was a barn. Several brown horses milled around a shady paddock. Through the trees just past the pool, Emily gazed at the blue expanse of Table Rock Lake.

If I had John Hackett's money, this is where I'd have built, too, Emily thought. But he seems like such a worm. There's just no justice.

A squeal from the tennis court was followed by the sound of a racket banging on concrete.

"I quit," yelled a slim blonde. Emily watched the cotton-candy mass of permed curls bounce as the pretty young woman stomped off the court and headed to a long table at the rear of the house where two chefs in tall white hats were handing glass plates to a line of people waiting to choose from piles of boiled shrimp set next to steaming silver chafing dishes. That's where they're hiding the collards and catfish, Emily thought. A silver tray of strawberries dipped in chocolate sweated in the summer heat. Next

16

to it, an ice sculpture of an upright fish dripped onto a tray of sliced melon and kiwis.

The young blonde in a white tennis dress approached a tuxedoed waiter, who poured her a glass of champagne. She slugged it back, and he poured another. Her tennis dress was one of a kind. Cut low in front, the white Lycra slid over her large breasts. Gold embroidery across what fabric was left announced Stella Love. Three-inch gold fringe swayed from the hem, not quite covering Miss Love's shapely behind.

Emily edged up to the group on the terrace where Stella Love was complaining that her tennis partner hogged the shots.

"He's a complete jerk," Stella said. Her shrill voice reminded Emily of the irate woman who had raised a fuss outside her cabin last night. Maybe the soon-to-be starlet was having a little affair at the Bitterroot. Emily vowed to find out what kind of car Stella drove and watch for it at the resort. Not that she was writing a tell-all story, but it would make her visit more interesting if she stumbled on a few local scandals.

"Well, he won't be hogging your shots come Friday," John Hackett boomed as he walked over to the group. He put a proprietary arm around Stella Love's shoulders and looked toward Emily. "My little star here's going to knock their socks off on Hot Country Friday, Miss Stone. You be sure to spell her name right," he said, fingering the sequins on the woman's breasts. Stella pushed his hand away and prattled on about the tennis game.

From above the lake came the sounds of a helicopter. Heads turned to watch the sleek white craft settle on the lawn, discharging a rotund man wearing denim overalls that glinted in the sun. Greeting other guests along the way, he approached the group where Emily stood. The man, probably about sixty, was at least six feet tall, with a gray beard and a bushy head of dark hair streaked with gray. No Grecian Formula here, Emily observed, glancing back at John Hackett's shining blue-black hairdo. The new arrival's overalls were studded here and there with rhinestones, and beneath the collar of his white shirt, a black string tie recalled old Western movie stars. As he shook hands with several people, Emily noticed his gleaming jewelry. A watch studded with turquoise chunks, a ring full of diamonds. Completing the fashion statement, the tip of a red bandana protruded from his overalls breast pocket.

"Dammit, Lyle, you just don't have enough money, do you?" John Hackett chided, pointing at the helicopter. "Nothing like a flashy arrival. But you'd better watch what you say, old boy. We got the press here. Miss Stone, you might not recognize our highflier. This is Lyle Malone, the richest hillbilly you ever met. Lyle started a theater in this town before it was a town. He's just kept growing every year, and laughing all the way to the trough." John's laugh turned into a coughing fit as he patted Lyle Malone's ample belly. "Lyle here's the host of Hot Country, and he's going to help my little Stella get rich and famous," John said.

Lyle ignored John Hackett's comments, but Emily noticed his eyes narrow slightly. Then the bearded man looked past John Hackett and his face lit up with a happy grin.

"Irene, darlin', how you been?" Lyle stepped past John to hug a thin woman wearing a pale blue sundress who had just walked up toward the group. So this was Irene Hackett. Emily had done her homework for this assignment by looking through dozens of back issues of the Branson newspaper. She'd read several accounts of parties thrown for visiting celebrities at what was called the Hackett estate. Stella Love's name had shown up in the accounts three weeks ago. But Irene was seldom mentioned.

She was apparently as reclusive as her husband was flamboyant. Recently, Emily had read two poems that Irene Hackett had allowed the newspaper to publish. The poetry had had a nice rhythm, but the work lacked confidence. Now Emily saw why. Irene's face was pretty in an innocent sort of way, as though she'd never been angry or had an ugly thought in her life. With most people, you could tell by the wrinkles and lines whether they had spent more time frowning or smiling, but Irene Hackett's face was like a blank mask. Her chin-length light brown hair was tucked behind her ears and her long, straight nose supported plain horn-rimmed glasses. It was hard to tell her age. Probably in her fifties too, and no sign of face-lifts. What a strange pair, she thought.

John Hackett watched Lyle hug his wife. Then, his arm still linked with Stella Love's, Hackett reached out and tousled his wife's hair. Before she could pull away, he slung his other arm around his wife's shoulders, nearly toppling her. "Lyle, did you know my little woman's writing poetry now? Maybe someday I'll make a star of her, too." John laughed. There was an uncomfortable silence, and Irene stood smiling meekly while Stella finished her glass of champagne.

"She's a damn good writer, and she doesn't need you to make her a star, Hackett," said a low, sultry voice from behind Irene. It was the high-heeled blonde who had grabbed Kenny Rogers from the stairway. In the sunshine, Emily could see the white concealer laid on a bit too heavily under her forty-something eyes.

Stella Love turned an icy gaze on the woman. "Monica, darling," she crooned, "maybe you ought to just stay in the background where you belong." Then Stella pulled away from John Hackett's grasp and headed toward the champagne table. With a noisy pat to Irene's bottom, John Hackett followed Stella's swinging fringe.

"Thanks, Monica," Irene said softly. "I'm going to get some tea." She turned and retreated to the house.

The blonde held out her hand to Emily. "I'm Monica Deal," she said. "I sing with Lyle. I'm one of his Goodtime Gals. And he's putting the wrong gal center stage on Friday." She turned to look in Stella Love's direction, then faced Lyle Malone. "I'd still like to know why you changed your mind and decided to knuckle under to John the Jerk." She stopped as if she wanted to say more, then thought better of it. "Lyle, don't you want some champagne?" She glanced toward the back of the house and saw John Hackett, his arm around Stella Love's waist, heading for the living room. "I see the air is clear at the bar now. I'll get you some."

From the pocket of his overalls, Lyle Malone produced a turquoise-encrusted silver flask and said to Monica, "Honey, I brought my own champagne. You want a swig?" As he held the open flask toward Monica, Emily smelled Southern Comfort, and her stomach rippled. She had been feeling too close to the past for days now, anticipating the trip to Branson. The smell of her father's favorite vintage was just too much.

"Would you excuse me?" Emily asked the group. She walked down the path toward a shady bench beneath a giant oak tree where she sat and gazed back at the crowd. Most of the women wore something with sequins. Young women in bathing suits wore high heels. Several men sported sleek, Western-cut suits—one baby-blue, one pink. One good-looking curly-haired man wore an elaborately painted cowboy shirt and jeans with dimes sewn down the side seams. All the men wore cowboy boots except the preppies on the tennis court. She spotted Mel Tillis, spiffy in a white suit and lavender boots. Emily had read that Tillis was doing some strenuous dance numbers in his new show. Apparently the exercise was paying off because he looked trim and healthy for his sixty years. Overall, the garb of the Branson crowd was stunning, if somewhat overdone. Tampa high society would die if they saw this party, Emily thought with a smile.

She gazed at the rear of the long two-story brick house. Lots of windows filled with plants. A balcony with a wooden railing extended the length of the second floor above the flagstone patio. Toward the left end of the balcony, nearly hidden from view by a tall hibiscus in a pot, John Hackett stood facing Stella Love, his arms around her waist. He had his face buried in her neck while Stella took a drink from the champagne glass. Emily looked around to see if any of the other guests had noticed them, but no one seemed to be looking in that direction. Might as well be nosy, Emily thought, and sauntered toward the house.

Across the living room, Emily spotted a library. No one was in the room, and she wandered along the rows of floor-to-ceiling shelves. The room smelled of leather from the books and a burgundy leather sofa with a matching pair of chairs. The room was beautiful; it reminded Emily of the picture cut from a magazine advertisement long ago that she had hanging above the computer in her apartment. It was her dream room. In the picture, a softly lit room was lined on three walls with bookshelves. Books lay strewn on Oriental rugs and a few, open perhaps to a special passage, rested on a tabletop beside lush house plants. In the center of the picture was the advertised item. It was a sort of double-bed-size chaise lounge that would accommodate two readers, each leaning against a backrest, legs stretched out, facing each other. Some nights while Emily sat at her computer trying to write a poem or catching up on an article that was due, she would look up at the picture and imagine herself in that dream library. She would select a worn volume from the shelves and settle down at her end of the lounger. Across from her, the man of her dreams smiled at her above his Melville. From time to time, he would read an especially good passage to her. Then he'd be absorbed again in his reading, and she would watch him, wondering if he even knew she existed while he read about bare-skinned women on South Sea islands. Just then, he would reach out to gently massage her feet while they both took their voyages to other worlds. Sometimes in her fantasy, it was Jim who sat with her, sometimes it was a faceless form she had yet to meet. The Hacketts' library resembled her dream only by virtue of the many volumes, and the smell of books.

On one wall of the library, small gas flames flickered behind the glass doors of a fireplace. Nice touch for a summer party, Emily thought. From one shelf, the glass eyes of a taxidermied fawn stared down at her. A brass plaque beside the fawn noted that it had been killed in a mowing accident in a hayfield. Emily turned away in disgust. On the coffee table, an elaborately bound copy of Browning's poems lay open to "Porphyria's Lover." Emily had a hard time imagining John Hackett reading.

Emily thought of Hackett on the balcony with Stella Love and remembered her reason for coming into the house. She was about to step out of the library when she saw Irene Hackett cross the hall and start up the broad staircase. Behind her, Lyle Malone softly cleared his throat.

"I hope you don't take our little bickering the wrong way, ma'am," he said. His large frame seemed to dwarf the shelves of books. "You know how us country folks can feud one day and fiddle together the next."

"I thought the Hatfields and McCoys were a thing of the past," Emily said. For some reason, she felt comfortable with this man; he was almost familiar, somehow. But, she reminded herself, let's remember I'm not always the best judge of character.

22

"Well, it's just John," Lyle was saying, staring at his unadorned brown leather boots. "He never wants people to know he inherited his money from his family. Maybe he's aware that some people think it's better to earn your own way. Whatever it is, he just gets a little high-handed sometimes. He's kind of taken Stella under his wing, and others—well, you know what sour grapes are. Monica's fit to be tied, but everything'll be all right come Friday because that's the last anyone's ever going to hear of Stella Love. Her singing voice is the only flat thing about that girl." Smile lines crinkled around his eyes and he adjusted his black string tie.

"If she's not good, why are you featuring her in the show?" Emily ask.

Lyle played with his tie again. "Well, you know, we're small-town folks here. We don't forget it if someone's done us a favor in the past. Sometimes the past can be kind of hard to forget." The smile wrinkles disappeared. "I settled in this town when Marvel Cave and good fishing were the only attractions. I've watched the woods give way to motels and theaters, and I've watched this beard turn gray." He pulled on his whiskers. "John's right when he says I've made a little money on all this progress. So has he, and so've a lot of others. But most of us work hard, too. It's really sweat that keeps the machinery greased."

Emily liked the rumble of this man's voice. He could give her insights into the growth here, she thought, but she wondered just how much she could get him to open up.

From one of the shelves, Lyle picked up a miniature violin and plucked a string. He pulled the eight-inch bow across the strings and got only an off-pitch shriek. "I don't mean to tell you your business, Miss Emily, but sometimes outsiders who come in here to watch us for a week get some wrong ideas. They think we're backward hicks. They think we're not trying to take care of our lakes and trees

23

during all this building boom, and they forget that part of what draws folks to come see us is our common roots.''

He replaced the violin on the shelf. "See, when country music started getting played on radio back in the thirties, people all over realized they'd all been singing about the same suffering. We was all poor, or heartbroke or lonely sometime in our life. When ol' Roy Acuff sang, it touched everybody. We learned we weren't all alone out there. That's what a country song still does for people, just lets them know the darkness of a night doesn't have to hurt.''

Lyle sucked his teeth. He pulled out the bandana, wiped sweat beads off his forehead, and glanced at the fireplace. Then he shook his head and looked back at Emily. "I'm sorry for raving at you that way. I'd just like people to know the truth about things here, that's all.''

"I'll do my best to tell the truth about Branson,'' Emily said. Somehow she felt that this was a man she wouldn't like to disappoint. "And I'd like to talk to you some more sometime this week about the town and the music, if that'd be all right.''

"Well, sure it would, darlin'.'' His smile lit a glow in his eyes. "You just come by the theater anytime. I think I'll go outside and find a cool breeze. Care to join me for a stroll?''

"No, thanks,'' Emily said. "I think I'll stroll to the ladies' room instead.'' She watched him walk away. There was a sadness to him, maybe just an oldness. But he was attractive too, in a way. It seemed to Emily that as she grew older an ever-widening range of men caught her eye. Well, I've never had a hillbilly singer, she thought. Might be interesting.

Again, Emily turned toward her mission upstairs. In the entry hall, the wide dark wood stairs led to the second floor. The young man who had given out name tags no longer sat at his post by the front door. The door stood slightly open to the circular driveway, lined with limousines and pickup trucks. "Pick-'em-up trucks," her father had called them. Through the door Emily saw Lyle, leaning against the far porch column, mopping his brow.

Emily climbed the stairs, and heard nothing but the band that had begun playing from a stage beside the pool. "Your cheatin' heart, will tell on you . . . ," someone crooned.

The second-floor hallway stretched in either direction from the stairs, rose carpeting leading past a dozen closed doors. She turned to the right and walked slowly, looking at framed photos of Branson's past. A muddy, unpaved Commercial Street in 1909, the ruins of the 1912 fire that destroyed all twenty stores downtown, a view of Powersite Dam under construction in 1913. She passed two doors leading to rooms that would face the back of the house and open onto the balcony. Each door bore a brass plaque. The first said Red Room, the second, Blue Room.

Infinitely creative, Emily noted. From behind the third, Green Room, she heard a giggle. She stopped and was pretending to examine another photo on the wall when she caught a movement out of the corner of her eye. Monica Deal stepped into view at the far end of the long hall. She halted when she saw Emily, turned, and went back into the room. Emily heard the door close softly. She waited a moment more, then took a few steps back to the Blue Room door and slowly turned the knob. She looked in, ready to say, "I'm sorry, Mrs. Hackett. I was looking for the bathroom."

No one was in the bedroom. She glanced around and felt sure she had seen the same room once in *Better Homes and Gardens*. The room looked as if no one had been inside since the decorator left. The fringe on the Oriental rug lay just so against the hardwood floor. The pale blue walls blended with the matching wallpaper and bed-spread. The drapes were nearly closed, letting in only a single shaft of sunlight. She quietly closed the door behind her and walked toward the wall of the adjoining room.

She picked up a small glass rabbit on the nightstand and nonchalantly looked it over. She scanned the room, looking for a place that might conceal a security camera, but there was only the paneled wood and modern oils, nondescript but color coordinated. With another glance toward the closed door, Emily pressed her ear to the wall.

"Oh, baby, I love your mouth," she heard John Hackett say. "So young. Lips like cherry wine, sweet thing. You keep on doing that and you'll never get old. I'm the fountain of youth, baby." A moment's silence, then she heard Stella laugh. "No, wait, baby," John said. "Come back here, honey."

"No more, you creep. That's it. I'm finished with this." Stella Love's voice was high-pitched and her words sounded slurred. Emily held her breath to hear. "You're limp as spaghetti, you impotent old fool," she said mockingly. "And anyway, my name's in lights now, and after Friday I'm not going to need a thing from you, not that you ever had much to give." She laughed. "You can just kiss my butt all the way to Nashville. Now go get me some champagne."

"Who do you think you are, ordering me around?" Hackett shouted.

"You either get champagne for me or I'll just go out on the balcony and announce to your guests that John the Stud has a little problem, a teeny weeny little problem." Emily heard Stella laugh, then the sound of movement in the room next to where she stood crouched. Maybe it was a chair scraping the floor. She darted for the door. A glance showed no one in the hall, and she closed the door silently behind her and quickly walked toward the stairs, then descended toward fresh air.

* * *

Behind her, she heard a door close upstairs, but she didn't look back.

Instead, she headed for the pool and the band. A nasty little Peyton Place seemed to lurk beneath the party's surface. She certainly wasn't naive, but she wasn't much into investigative journalism, either. At least not on such a personal level. Her heart pounded a little from what she had overheard and from the risk she'd taken. Helping herself to a glass of champagne from a tray in the living room, Emily walked toward an empty chair by the pool. Most of the guests were gathered around the bandstand watching a bearded fiddler playing "Orange Blossom Special" while lying on his back.

The scream cut through the fiddle tune like microphone feedback. Heads whirled toward the sound, toward the champagne table where a waitress screamed again. Stella Love lay on her back on the flagstones below the balcony. Her mouth was open. Her eyes were open. Dark blood flowed from beneath the blond hair and spread across the stones.

Emily glanced up at the empty balcony. Then she saw John Hackett come through the living room door. His face was gray. He stared at the body. When he looked out at the stunned, motionless crowd, his gaze rested on Emily.

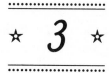

★ 3 ★

A hundred people were silent and still as Hackett walked to Stella's fallen form. He knelt beside her and lifted her lifeless hand, cupping it in both of his.

Monica Deal came through the living room doors and saw the scene. "No!" she screamed and rushed toward Stella. Lyle Malone was right behind her and grabbed her, turning her toward him before she could throw herself on Stella's bleeding body. Other men rushed over. "Stay back," a young man said, pushing John Hackett away from the body. He felt for a pulse in Stella's neck, lowered his ear to her chest and listened for a long moment, gesturing for silence. The crowd was motionless again. Then the young man passed his hand over Stella's face, pushing the lids over her sightless eyes. "Somebody better call the sheriff," he said as a buzz of conversation rose from the shocked guests.

People were moving toward the living room doors, but Emily edged closer to where Stella lay. She was stunned. She swallowed the knot of bile in her throat while an image of the only other dead body she'd ever seen swam into her mind. Everyone at her father's funeral had said how peaceful he looked, lying against the coffin's white satin ticking. Emily had refused to believe it was her father. She was convinced, as a ten-year-old in shock might be, that the familiar figure in the casket was only a wax dummy people used at funerals. She had stared at the waxen image of her father, watching for signs of life, the faint beginnings of a smile or the sudden burst of a grin like when he felt a fish tug on his line. But her mother had taken her hand and led her away from the casket, and as they walked into the street in front of the funeral home, Emily scanned the crowd to see if her father was there, secretly waiting to surprise her. Sometimes, in a large crowd, Emily would still catch herself scanning the faces while the image of her father came to mind. Now Emily saw a wax figure that had been Stella Love.

Lyle Malone handed the crying Monica into a nearby woman's care and bent over the body. He spread his red bandana across Stella's face. Blood matching the bandana still oozed from beneath her head, running across the stone and dripping slowly onto the second step.

Emily saw the crowd of people moving toward the back of the house stop their progress and clear a path. Irene Hackett came out. When John saw her, he rushed toward her and grabbed her, turning her back toward the house. "Don't look, baby," he said. "There's been a terrible accident. Just come back inside."

Emily saw Irene stop. She pulled away from John and took several steps toward the dead body. One hand came up to her mouth, the other fluttered in the direction of John as though warding off a blow. Silently, she looked at her husband, then around at the crowd and back toward where the blood dripped onto her wide stone steps. Emily thought later that Irene hadn't walked back into the house; it had looked more as though the diminutive woman were drifting without moving her feet. Like the Wicked Witch of the East, doused by a bucket of water,

Irene shrank from Emily's view. No one said a word, but Monica broke away from the woman who was holding her and ran toward the house after Irene. Several people in the crowd, startled by Monica's flight, also headed toward the door.

"I think you all better wait a minute," said a tall, heavyset man wearing a tan uniform who emerged from the living room. "Let's everyone just stay where you are, please." He held out his hands as if inviting a congregation to prayer.

Sheriff Ron Turner, followed by a young, pimply-faced deputy, came over to the body. "What happened here?" he asked. John Hackett joined him.

"I'm afraid we let Stella have a little too much champagne, Ron," Hackett said. "She was upstairs and she must have lost her balance on the balcony."

John Hackett moved close to the sheriff and spoke quietly, but not so quietly that Emily couldn't hear his warning. "Ron, we've got a newspaper reporter here from Florida. She's the one over there in the tan jacket and white dress. We might want to be a little careful about what's said."

Emily saw Hackett and the sheriff look at her. Then Sheriff Turner straightened his shoulders and glanced at the quiet crowd who stood watching him. He nodded to John.

"Folks, it looks like we've had a little accident here," Sheriff Turner said. "The coroner's going to be here soon, so why don't you all just find a place in the shade, and Mike and I will be around to talk to everyone." The sheriff pulled a notebook out of his back pocket.

"John, why don't we go inside?"

As John Hackett and the sheriff walked toward the living room, Emily pulled herself out of her shock and ambled in the same direction. Others began to gather in small groups, talking in hushed tones and glancing toward where Stella Love still lay with the red bandana on her face. At an umbrella-shaded table, Lyle Malone sat by himself, staring toward the body. He didn't move as Emily walked by, watching him from the corner of her eye.

Inside the cool living room, Sheriff Turner and John Hackett sat on a sofa. Emily walked to a table and helped herself to a glass of iced tea. She looked around and saw no one in the room smoking except Hackett. Bad time to bum a cigarette, she thought with regret, and wandered out to the front hall. From there, Emily could see into the kitchen where Monica Deal sat at the table, her head resting on her folded arms, shoulders moving with her silent sobs. Irene was beside her, patting her back. Emily wandered closer to the kitchen door.

"Monica, it wasn't your fault," Emily heard Irene Hackett say. "There wasn't a thing you could have done. You tried to straighten her out, but she was too far gone. You know that. You said yourself last week that she was headed for a fall. You just didn't know what kind. Monica, stop. You can't blame yourself, honey," Irene soothed.

Monica raised her head and swiped at her face with a handful of tissues. She saw Emily standing near the doorway, turned and rose quickly and went into a room off the kitchen and closed the door. Irene looked up at Emily. As before, Emily could read no expression on Irene's face, and she wondered if Irene had heard the exchange in the bedroom upstairs a few minutes ago, too.

Emily walked into the large white-tiled kitchen. Except for a few empty party glasses, nothing was out of place. Not a crumb or spill anywhere. Every picture was straight, every one of the numerous expensive knick-knacks was angled just so. Shining copper cookware hung from a rack above what appeared to be an unused stove-top.

"I'm so sorry this happened, Mrs. Hackett," Emily said, approaching the table. "I know everyone's very upset. What an awful thing to have happen." She pulled out a chair and sat across from Irene without waiting for an invitation. Emily detected a determined look in the woman's face, a certain movement of her jaw and a glint in her gray eyes that was not a reflection of the sunshine coming through the kitchen window.

"Well, this looks like a field day for a reporter, doesn't it?" Irene asked in a quiet voice. "I hope you're not planning to blow this accident up into some sort of scandal. I was out in the stable checking on the horses when it happened, and I was planning to suggest to John when I got back that we start encouraging some coffee and iced tea. I thought some of the guests, including Stella, were getting a little out of hand." Irene Hackett picked a piece of lint off the dark blue place mat centered on the glass-topped table. "But who could have known the poor little bird would try to fly off that balcony." There was a long pause. Emily recalled seeing Irene going upstairs before Lyle came into the library. Was she really in the stable when Stella fell?

Emily sat motionless while Irene looked down at her finger tracing a circle on the tabletop. "You know, she wasn't the most stable person," Irene volunteered. "Monica knew her quite well, and she'd been worried about her. It's so ironic with her career just getting off the ground and all. I'm sure you can understand why we're all so upset." Now Irene Hackett's hands were clenched into fists in front of her, the pearly knuckles contrasting with the first signs of liver spots.

"Of course," Emily said, remembering what she had heard just minutes before Stella's fall. "You know I'm here to cover the show. I'm not a gossip columnist as your husband seems to think, Mrs. Hackett. I'm sure you and Mr.

Hackett were both very fond of Stella," she lied, looking for a reaction. "I gather that your husband had helped her a great deal."

"Yes," Irene said in a level, noncommittal tone. "He enjoys helping people get started in business. It's always been his hobby." She glanced beyond Emily and closed her mouth. Emily saw a fleeting expression pass over Irene's face before the carefully woven mask returned. The look might have been fear.

Emily turned to see Sheriff Turner standing in the doorway looking at Irene.

"Excuse me, Irene," he said quietly. "Could I talk to you for a minute?"

Just then, John Hackett pushed past the sheriff and strode across the room to his wife, taking her hand. "If you'll excuse my wife, ma'am," Hackett said to Emily. "She's had quite a shock. Why don't you go lie down, honey, and I'll have someone bring you a cup of tea," Hackett said to Irene.

Irene stood to face him and for a moment they stared at each other. Irene glanced toward the sheriff. Then John Hackett patted his wife's shoulder. Emily felt a coldness in the room like the chilly breath that rushes out of a meat locker when the door swings open. Without a word, Irene Hackett left Emily seated at the table and traced Monica Deal's path of retreat.

"I apologize for all the commotion," Hackett said, turning a charming smile on Emily. "Sheriff Turner said he wouldn't be needing to talk to you, so if you'll excuse us, I'll plan to see you at the theater on Friday if not before." Hackett waited for Emily to stand up.

Emily took the hint and stood. "Yes," she said. "I'll plan to see you again." Emily barely managed a smile as she offered her hand to Hackett, who shook it briefly as though he were touching something hot. She looked again at the misshapen black pupil before she turned to walk back into the entry hall. She glanced back and saw he was still looking at her.

The elaborately carved front door was closed now. A few empty name tags lay scattered on the marble floor. She glanced into the living room where the sheriff stood with Lyle Malone. The sheriff glanced her way and stopped talking momentarily. Malone also looked in her direction. Well, I seem to have captured a lot of attention, Emily thought. I'm out of here. She turned the brass knob and was glad to escape into the warm fresh air.

As she headed down the circular drive to her car, Emily felt a wave of anger envelop her. The Ozarks don't disappoint, do they? she thought. The glitter doesn't hide the sleaze for long. I ought to just get in the car and leave this state. Let them send someone else up Friday. I've got all the background I need from here.

Emily slammed the car door and started the engine. The radio came on too loud, Tammy Wynette belting out "Stand By Your Man." She snapped it off and turned the air-conditioner fan to high.

As she turned out of the driveway, Emily saw a young girl standing across the road from the Hacketts' house. She might have been about six or seven, and wore jeans with a tear in one knee. The girl's blond hair hung in tangled strands and she rubbed one cheek with the back of her hand. She waved as Emily pulled out of the driveway. Emily waved back and then saw the child's T-shirt. I ♥ Country Music, it said. "Geez!" Emily groaned and roared off down the road. "Get me out of here."

A mile later, when she was back at the county highway, Emily pulled into a gas station and convenience store. Forcing herself not to think about it, she bought a six-pack of Bud Dry and a pack of Benson and Hedges Deluxe Ultra Light menthols. She had always enjoyed the long name of her favorite brand. She paid for them and didn't encourage the clerk's friendly chitchat. "Need a lighter?" he asked. In the car, she peeled open the cigarette pack and put one in her mouth. It felt strange and she threw it out the open window, but then she put another between her lips and pushed in the car's cigarette lighter. She started the engine and waited for the lighter to pop, then lit the cigarette quickly and sucked in a long draw. The second drag brought on the familiar light-headed feeling and the twinge of pain in her lungs. The dependance, one psychologist had told her, sprang from her feelings of abandonment over her father's early death. Be that as it may, Emily thought, this lack of willpower springs from my stupidity. She took one more drag and threw the lit cigarette out the window. Then she dropped the pack out the window too, and pulled out, angry at her lack of resolve.

It was nearly five in the afternoon. Emily felt too upset to return to the solitary cabin at the resort, so she turned toward a sign pointing to the old downtown section of Branson. The downtown was picturesque, three blocks lined by two-story buildings of stone or brick, most of an early 1900s vintage. Antique-looking street lamps had been added and from each one hung a basket of flowers, some pink, some white. It was charming. How pleasant to see a downtown area that had not become rundown as business expanded away from the older part of town. Emily drove slowly along the street, partly to look at the shop windows and partly to avoid hitting the tourists who crowded the sidewalks and seemed oblivious to traffic as they wandered across the street. Emily was fascinated by the window of Dick's Old-fashioned Five and Dime Store. She knew from her reading that the place had been built and continuously operated since the early 1930s. Every inch of window-display space was filled with knickknacks, faded plastic Memorial Day wreaths, Christmas decorations, rakes and hoes, and a variety of toys. "Everything you couldn't find anyplace else," the slogan read. Emily promised herself she would come back another day when it wasn't so crowded.

Just past the cluster of downtown shops, Emily saw a sign for Rocky's Italian Food down a side street and turned in that direction, thinking that a cool gin and tonic sounded good. A few cars were parked in front of the homey rustic building. It was dark inside after the sunlight of late afternoon, and Emily's eyes had to adjust to the dimness. But she felt herself relax as the familiar scents of beer, garlic, and last night's smoke settled around her. She sat at a small table in the corner. Half a dozen men and a pair of women sat at other tables. She ordered her drink from the waitress and leaned back, looking around and listening.

"Well, she could have fallen over that railing, as drunk as she was," said a man at a nearby table. "She almost fell on her ass on the tennis court. Did you see her?"

"No, I missed that," the other man said. "But I'll bet there are a few private celebrations going on tonight. Ol' Irene sure won't mind that she's out of the way. And what about Monica? Did you see her carrying on? Hell of an actress, eh? I'll bet either of them would have liked to throw a shindig seeing Stella lying there like that."

Emily didn't recognize them from the party. It's probably just the way rumors spread in small towns, she told herself. She had come here to escape thoughts of the party, so she tried to tune out the men's conversation. The drink was cold and strong with gin, just the way she liked it. She had just leaned back and run her fingers through her hair when she glanced up at the door as it opened. It was hard to see the features of the man who came into the lounge because the sunlight streaming through the door behind him made him a dark silhouette, but as the door closed, she recognized her handsome cowboy neighbor from the Bitterroot. Emily looked down at her drink, hoping he wouldn't notice her.

"Hey, there, ma'am. Remember me?"

Too late. Emily smiled up at Robert Simmons, who was already pulling out a chair across from her.

"Mind if I join you? It's time for a cold one. I been out in the sun too much today," he said.

"Sure," Emily said politely.

Robert Simmons was a beauty, tanned and slim, probably not yet thirty. Today he wore a Western-cut shirt, dark teal-blue, unbuttoned just enough so a patch of dark chest hair showed: no gold chains. She liked his hairstyle, neat and trim on the sides, but still with the charm of long hair. She remembered the times she had tried to talk Jim into letting his hair grow long, but he said it didn't match his image of himself. Maybe visiting with this guy would be an interesting diversion. She hoped he hadn't heard about Stella's fatal fall from grace.

The waitress came; Simmons ordered a Budweiser. Emily caught herself wondering how it would feel to kiss his full lips. What is it that I find so attractive about men who seem a little offbeat? Emily asked herself. Through her memory paraded an array of old boyfriends: the motorcycle nut who nearly killed her teaching her to ride his dirt bike; the handsome dark-eyed poet who had a nervous breakdown one night in their second month of dating; the brilliant chemist who liked her cooking so much he gained thirty pounds in six months before deciding to become a vegetarian. At least they weren't boring. Then she thought of Jim. It wasn't that he was dull. He just liked normal things like baseball and stock-car races. She was often grateful for the stability and balance he brought to her life. Then she looked across the table at Robert Simmons as he took a long pull from his beer. Not a cowboy, she told herself. You definitely don't need a cowboy.

"So what'd you do today?" He set down his beer and flashed a smile at Emily. "Did you have an interesting time?"

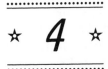

★ 4 ★

Robert Simmons had an easy Southern way of talking. His drawl was soft and comfortable as old leather. When he asked Emily if she'd stay and eat dinner with him, he had made her smile by saying: "Oh, come on, darlin'. Give me a chance. I'll treat you so many ways you'll just be bound to like one of them."

When she had nearly finished her second gin and tonic, and Robert was on his third Bud, Emily excused herself to go to the ladies' room. She looked at herself in the mirror, pushed back her hair, and wiped at a smudge of eyeliner. All right, she told herself. I'll have dinner with him. He's different, but he seems like a nice guy. No harm in having dinner. I have to eat anyway.

With that decided, they ordered fried ravioli appetizers in a sauce that must have been made with jalapeño peppers, enough to make their eyes water; Robert said he felt as if he were home in Texas. Halfway through the spaghetti and meatballs, after he'd told her about his happy childhood, his wonderful grandmother who had helped raise him, his wild-hare stint in St. Petersburg where he had not exactly owned a construction company but had indeed done roofing when it was 104 degrees, and the rattlesnake roundup he had photographed from the safety of his car, he asked Emily what she did.

He was quiet and sipped his beer while Emily briefly told him about her job. As she explained about being a reporter, about coming to Branson to do a story, she saw a subtle change in her young companion's body language. Simmons straightened slightly and leaned back a little in his chair. It was a small drawing away. And it wasn't the first time Emily had sensed that some men were at least surprised and then put off when they found out she was a professional with a career. She thought Simmons suddenly found her a bit less suitable for conquest. Even among professional men she met, the revelation sometimes had a negative effect. It was a reaction that disappointed Emily, but amused her too in a way. Jim's reaction had been just the opposite. He had leaned toward her, said "Really?" with interest, and had immediately asked her what kinds of assignments she found most interesting.

Even after so many years, Emily still wasn't sure if it was the fact that she worked, that she probably earned more than some of the men she met, or that her job as a reporter implied that she was innately nosy or inclined to uncover secrets leading to sensational stories. Often in conversation even with fairly close friends, Emily found herself assuring people that she wasn't "on the job" at that moment and that whatever they said wouldn't end up in print. When she finished her job description, Robert said, "Married? Got kids?"

His next unspoken questions were apparent to Emily: "Want to take care of me? Wash my socks? Manage my life? Buy me things? Take care of my elderly mother?" Emily took another bite of ravioli, wondering as she did why exactly she bothered with men.

While Emily took time to chew, before she'd had a chance to answer his questions about marriage and children, Simmons took up the story of his life where he had left off. Emily turned her thoughts toward Jim again. Jim wasn't like this. She thought of him as a nineties man, bright, fair, considerate of the rights of everyone. Still, she knew that even Jim liked to label things and thought automatically of the traditional roles for a wife, mother, breadwinner. But it wasn't because of bias. It sprang more from his desire for order and efficiency. Jim was a pretty independent kind of guy, but careful, cautious. He was the kind of guy who never tossed a pair of socks in his underwear drawer by mistake. But then neither did Emily, at least not often.

Robert Simmons was talking about the trouble he was having finding work in Branson. "People here have a chip on their shoulders against Texans, you know?" he said. Emily took a bite of garlic bread and tuned him out. When she got together with Jim in the evenings, they didn't spend long hours unloading the problems of the day on each other. They both had days when the job was a pain, or a co-worker had been a jerk, but when Emily saw Jim, what she wanted was escape, pleasant times, relaxation. "I'll be sympathetic and supportive to a point," she'd told Jim. "But no one really wants to carry another person's weight unless they've got a serious martyr complex."

"Want dessert?" Robert Simmons's question snapped Emily back to reality. She settled for coffee with a shot of Kahlua and wished Simmons was a smoker. After coffee, he suggested she go with him to the Downhill Club where there was a country band and a two-step contest tonight. Thinking it might be fun, and provide some material for her story, Emily agreed.

When they got to the parking lot, Simmons suggested they take his pickup to the club, offering to bring her back to her car later. "That parking lot is always crowded," he said. "It'll be better if we're in one car."

Emily agreed again, against her better judgment. Inside the pickup, Emily felt as if she were back in high school. A pair of fuzzy dice dangled from his rearview mirror. The Land That Time Forgot, Emily thought, complete with Neanderthals.

But Simmons was right about the parking. The club's tiny lot was overflowing and they had to park nearly a block away as it was. It was smoky inside and packed with men in cowboy hats and young women in jeans and sparkling shirts. The club was small, but there were at least fifty couples on the dance floor, moving in a circular pattern with smooth, gliding steps. Some of the couples threw in frequent complicated spins. Emily knew they were dancing the two-step. She'd seen it on Country Music Television while flicking through channels, but she didn't have a clue how to do the dance, and declined Robert's invitation to dance. At Emily's urging he asked another woman to dance and put on an impressive display. Emily promised Robert that she would try it another time, then told him she needed to get back to the resort soon since she had a lot of work to do the following day.

"Well, if this isn't your thing, darlin'," Robert said, slipping his arm around her neck, "let's head across the street. They've got a rhythm-and-blues band over there and I hear they're from Texas. That means they're good." He grinned.

"All right," Emily said. "But just for a few minutes."

Across the street, the Copper Penny was packed, too. Most of the people in this crowd appeared to be about Emily's age, and they weren't dressed in the glittery country style she'd seen at the other club. Emily was surprised and pleased to see so many people turn out for rhythm and blues. She had not expected such diversity of music here, and remembered seeing a sign at Rocky's advertising a jazz combo on Mondays. But it made sense. Many professional musicians with backgrounds in a variety of styles must be attracted to work in the shows in Branson.

This was Emily's kind of music. They found a small table near the back of the room. A good-looking waiter promptly took their orders and returned with cold beers.

Emily was feeling the effects of the drinks, and when the band started a slow rendition of "When a Man Loves a Woman," she accepted Robert's invitation to dance. She liked the way he danced and didn't mind that he held her tightly against him. They stayed for another half hour, during which Robert was attentive, keeping an arm around her shoulders or holding her hand. It made Emily a little nervous. And she was getting tired. It was nearly midnight when Emily finally convinced Robert to drive her back to her car.

He drove slowly back to Rocky's parking lot and pulled up beside her car. He got out of the pickup and came around to open the door for her, although she was halfway out when he got to her side. As she unlocked her car door and turned to thank him for the evening, he took her face in both his hands and kissed her gently on the lips. Emily felt herself melting inside.

"I think I'd better go, Robert," Emily said when he released her mouth. "Thank you. I had a wonderful time."

"So did I, darlin'," he drawled. "Let's do it again. How about if I meet you at six o'clock on Monday at Rocky's? We can have dinner and listen to some more jazz."

Emily agreed to the date, and Robert gave her a light kiss on her cheek. "You just remember that I'll be right next door tonight. If your bed gets too cold, I'll save you a hot spot." He grinned.

Emily was smiling when she pulled out of Rocky's. Her head buzzed a little from the liquor, but mostly it was the kisses that had pleased her. She had only had a couple of dates with other men since she met Jim, and it felt good to know she was still desirable. And Simmons was so good-looking. She thought about the warm spot in his bed and quickly decided that would be a serious mistake. Still, it had its appeal. God, she thought, I just have no spine at all.

Arriving at the resort at the same time as Robert could make for an awkward scene, so Emily decided to take a ride out past the Hacketts' to see if there was any activity at the house.

Table Rock's water looked black in the dim moonlight; calm, foreboding. How fast would a body sink in that water? Maybe driving by the Hacketts' wasn't such a good idea. She was afraid she'd probably have nightmares tonight anyway. As she approached the mansion, Emily expected to see floodlights illuminating the grand yard, but the grounds and the house were dark. No lights showed in any window. She slowed down for a good look, and as she picked up speed again, her headlights shone on a woman's figure walking along the road toward the house. As she neared, she could see it was Irene Hackett. Irene was wearing a dark-colored jogging suit, a dangerous thing to wear for a nighttime walk along the road. Then Emily realized that few cars would be out on this road at this time of night. Emily slowed and rolled down her window and called to Irene, who was walking briskly on the other side of the road.

"Irene, hello, it's Emily Stone, the reporter," Emily called. The woman continued to walk, not even looking in her direction. "Irene?" Emily called louder. "Are you all right?" The woman never broke her stride and turned into the circular drive without a backward glance. Emily saw her go into the house and close the door. Still, no lights came on in the house.

How odd, Emily thought. Swell night for a stroll with ghosts still lurking. I wonder why she didn't speak to me. Probably just doesn't like the nosy press, like everyone else in this town.

Emily headed back to the Bitteroot. Now she was really tired. A warm bath would be just the thing to finish off the day. What a day it had been. The events at the Hacketts' party could be inspiration for a country song. "She jumped off the balcony because the cowboy wouldn't dance. . . ." That's not funny, she chided herself.

Inside the Hacketts' house, Irene turned on a small lamp in the kitchen and filled the copper teakettle. She lit the burner and sat down at the table. She folded her arms on the table and put her head down on them. John walked quietly from the dark hallway into the circle of light.

"Are you all right?" he asked.

Irene lifted her head and looked around at him. "Yes. Are you?"

John stood above her. "I'm fine," he said. The kettle began making gurgling sounds.

"Want tea?" Irene asked.

"Thanks." John took a cup from the cupboard, set it on the counter by the stove, and sat down at the table.

Irene got up and from the same cupboard took out another cup, and two tea bags. She was standing by the stove with her back to John when he slammed his fists against the table. Irene jumped and spun to look at him.

John had put his head on the table, his face in his hands. Irene said nothing. The teakettle whistled and Irene shut off the burner and poured the water into the cups. She poked at the tea bags with a spoon.

She flinched when John stood up suddenly from the table. He began to pace around the room, Irene watching him.

"It shouldn't have happened," John said. His voice broke. "It just didn't have to happen like that. I was going to go get her more champagne. I was about to leave, but I went back out to the balcony. I shouldn't have gone back, should I?" John picked up a glass figurine of a dove and hurled it across the room. It shattered on the tile floor. Irene went to him and took hold of his arm.

"John," she said sharply. "Calm down. Sit down and drink your tea." She led him back to the table where he slumped in a chair. She put the teacup down in front of him and stood by the counter again. The clink of her spoon against the cup was the only sound.

"You have to forget what happened today," Irene said. "You have to put it out of your mind forever. I don't want you to talk about it again, John. Anyone could see she was drinking too much. And I know, we both know, how belligerent she could get."

"She was crazy. You know she was losing it."

"I know. It was just the drinking."

"No," John said. "It was more than that. She was a sick girl. I should never have tried to help her."

"You couldn't have known, John. She seemed like a nice girl at first." She took a drink of the steaming tea. "Drink your tea. You did everything you could for her. I should have gotten closer to her, but she was always so distant with me, like I didn't even live here, like I was her servant or something."

Irene sat back down at the table. "You want something to eat?"

"No," he said. "Let's go to bed."

Irene hesitated. "I'm still kind of wound up. Why don't you go on."

"We haven't slept together in a month now," John said, running his hand over his slick hair. "Don't you think we ought to try it again sometime?"

"Don't worry so much about it, John. You don't have to prove anything to me, you know. I've been your wife a long time." After a moment she looked at him and said, "But I do wish you'd call Dr. Robinson and make an appointment. Just get a check-up so you'll know that nothing's wrong."

John stood up suddenly. The kitchen chair fell over backward. He grabbed it and set it down hard. Irene held her teacup in both hands. "I don't need to see Dr. Robinson to know what's wrong! What I need is a little peace!"

He headed toward the hallway.

"Where are you going?" Irene called, raising her voice so it sounded shrill. "It's too late to go out. You need some rest."

She heard the front door slam, heard the car start in the driveway and pull away. Irene put down the teacup, turned off the lamp in the kitchen, and went upstairs in the dark. She passed the door marked "Green Room" without a glance. In her own room, Irene turned on a lamp and took a small leather-covered journal out of the nightstand drawer and sat down at the writing desk. Pen poised, she stared at the blank sheet.

Emily drove slowly along the county road leading to the resort's driveway. She knew she'd had too much to drink, and the road seemed more winding at night than it had in the daylight. There had been little traffic on the strip. The clubs didn't close down until one A.M., and the tourists had long been in bed since most of the shows let out around ten P.M. It had felt strange to be able to drive at the speed limit past the empty, neon-lit theaters.

As she drove along the dark road, Emily, glancing in her rearview mirror noticed a car coming up fast behind her, with its bright beams on. Now she had to maneuver the unfamiliar curves even more carefully with the headlights' glare reflecting in her mirrors. She switched the rearview mirror to its night position, but that didn't help much. One of the car's headlights was misaligned, so the light from behind was still blinding Emily.

The creep. What's the matter with him? Probably drunk. More drunk than I am.

As she slowed for a curve, she tapped her brakes, hoping the red lights would make the driver following her back off. But it didn't. The other car stayed right on her tail. Emily saw the road straighten and kept her slow pace, hoping he would pass, but too quickly another curve appeared. He must be more familiar with the road than she was. On the next hill, Emily picked up a little speed. So did the car behind her. Then she tried her technique of slowing way down, creeping along at about twenty miles per hour, hoping the driver in back would become so annoyed he'd finally pass. That didn't work, either. The car stayed with her. Suddenly, Emily's annoyance gave way to fear. It was a dark road. She knew she would pass few houses on the way to the resort. What if it was a mugger waiting for his opportunity to stop her car and rob her, or worse. Emily checked to be sure the car doors were locked. She decided to drive as fast as she could to get to the resort, and she stepped on the accelerator. The car behind her kept pace, taking each turn just as Emily did. Now she was clutching the steering wheel tightly, leaning forward, squinting to see as much as she could of the oncoming curves in her own bright beams. The sign for Scenic View told Emily she was getting close to the resort's turnoff: she had stopped there on her way out to watch the sun setting over the valley far below. It was a long lefthand curve and Emily took it as fast as she could. She could feel her car's wheels straining to hold to the pavement, and she heard the tires squeal as she entered the curve. That was the moment the car behind her chose to pass. She saw the headlights pull out to her left and heard the roar of a big engine alongside her car. Emily kept her eyes on the road ahead, holding her car into the curve, afraid that decelerating now might lose the momentum she needed to stay on the road. Then she saw the front fender of the other car. It was almost touching her car. The other car seemed to be matching her speed, edging toward her. He's trying to run me off the road, Emily realized in panic.

48

She glanced quickly at the car beside her, but couldn't see the driver, only the shiny blackness of the car's side inches away, edging closer and a little ahead, beginning to cut in front of her. Emily hit the brakes, too hard at first, and felt her back wheels begin to skid toward the cliff's edge and the valley below. It all happened so fast that later Emily didn't know how she had thought to let off the brakes, but she did. Her car slowed, righted itself from the sideways skid. The black car sped past until its taillights disappeared over the next hill. Emily slowed her car to a crawl. She was shaking all over. Gradually her fear gave way to anger, and she cussed the driver all the way to the turn-off to Bitterroot, vowing to be more cautious the next time some carload of drunken rednecks was following her.

She was still trembling when she pulled into the parking place for her cabin. Robert's black pickup truck was parked near his cabin. No lights came from inside. Quietly, she closed her car door and walked to the cabin's porch. As she reached the door, something small and white moved toward her foot. Emily let out a small shriek and jumped back. In the dim light, she saw it was a tiny fluffball of a kitten. The kitten mewed and rubbed its face on Emily's foot. "Oh, you sweet thing," Emily said and reached down to rub the kitten's ears. It was bedraggled, underfed, with clumps of mud dried to its fur here and there.

"Well, can't hurt if you come in for a little while," Emily cooed, reaching to pick up the cat. But at her touch, the kitten jumped and ran into the shadows toward the rear of her car. Emily unlocked the cabin door, turned on the light, and took a small flashlight from the nightstand, remembering the creatures who had upended the trash cans the night before. She went back out and shone the flashlight toward her car, hoping Robert wasn't awake. Walking behind the cars, she heard a squeak from the direction of Robert's truck. Emily panned the flashlight's beam and saw something gleam in the road near Robert's cabin. She walked toward the sparkle and saw a scrap of gold fabric covered in sequins. As Emily bent to pick it up, she thought of Stella Love, the sequined tennis dress crumpled around her dead body. Emily remembered the vicious epithets of the angry woman outside her cabin the night before. Could that have been Stella? Emily wondered. Who was she visiting out here?

Then she saw the kitten, sitting meekly by the rear of Robert's truck. Emily crouched and tried to lure it with the shiny fabric. The kitten couldn't resist and when it was within reach, Emily grabbed it, held it tightly, talking softly about what good friends they would soon become as she carried it into the cabin. She picked off the mud on the kitten's coat. "See how clean and fluffy you are?" When Emily put the kitten down, she walked around, exploring and making little leaps each time it encountered a shoe or some other item on the floor.

"Sorry I don't have any milk, Fluffy. But if you come back tomorrow I'll see that I'm properly stocked." Emily hung up her clothes and ran the bathwater while the kitten played with a tassel on Emily's robe. As Emily soaked in the warm water, Fluffy sat on the edge of the tub, watching the ripples in the water intently, as if it expected a mouse to emerge. When Emily was dry, she gave Fluffy a good snuggle, said good night, and set the little furball outside the door. For several minutes she almost gave in to the plaintive mews from beyond the door. Instead, she turned on the television to David Letterman and quickly fell asleep.

★ **5** ★

When Emily woke up Sunday morning, she couldn't think where she was for a moment. Then Stella Love's bleeding head filled her memory like a close-up shot on a movie screen and she groaned and rolled over. I'm in Branson. Land of tourists and dead people. Then the thought of the kitten made Emily smile and she donned her robe and opened the door. "Kitty, kitty?" she called quietly, and while she observed that Robert Simmons's truck was still there, she saw no sign of the kitten. Disappointed, Emily went back inside, and put on her navy silk blouse with pin-striped slacks. She had planned a drive into the countryside for today. As she dressed, she remembered the black car nearly running her off the cliff the night before. Just an isolated incident, she told herself. No reason to get spooked.

Emily also planned to stop by the sheriff's department. She didn't expect Sheriff Turner to be there on a Sunday morning, but she hoped someone else would be able to give her a copy of the report on Stella Love's death.

Breakfast was decaf and an Egg McMuffin on her way downtown. According to her town map, the sheriff's department was just outside city limits but within blocks of the city's downtown police station. She found the old stone building with a sign reading Taney County Sheriff's Department hanging in front. Over the door, set into the stones, a plaque read 1910. A planter beside the door held a brilliant profusion of marigolds and impatiens. The lobby was small and had obviously changed little since the building was built. Against one wall, metal grilles of three bank-teller cages remained. A fourth cage had been replaced by a glass window that read Information. The lobby was clean and tidy except for an overflowing ashtray beside an orange Naugahyde couch.

"Is Sheriff Turner in?" she asked a uniformed desk clerk who sat behind the glass window. The clerk was a fiftyish woman, chunky and graying. She put down her *USA Today* without a smile.

"I'll see," she said. "And you are . . . ?"

"Emily Stone. I'm a reporter for the *Tampa Tribune.*" Emily watched the woman's eyebrows lift just a little. Without a word, the woman got up and walked down a short hall. Emily saw her standing outside a door, talking to someone in the room.

As Emily waited, she looked at Wanted posters on the bulletin board. I bet they all live around here, Emily thought.

Sheriff Turner came into the reception area. He had on a gray Pittsburgh Steelers T-shirt and a pair of khaki shorts that rode low under his belly. He needed a shave. Emily guessed he'd very soon be home drinking beer and watching football.

"What can I do for you, ma'am?" the sheriff asked, forgoing any kind of greeting.

"I'm Emily Stone, a reporter for the *Tampa Tribune.* I'm here working on a story about Branson, and happened to be at the Hacketts' yesterday when Stella Love was killed. I stopped by to see the report on her death."

"Well, ma'am, we release our reports once a week for

the press. You can come by next Friday." He turned to go. Emily was taken aback by his attitude. Picking up police reports was standard practice in Tampa. They were considered public information, and unless someone got behind on duties, the reports were always waiting. She reminded herself where she was and tried a different tack. Sometimes a little coquettishness worked well and Emily was not beneath putting feminine wiles to work—within reason.

"Wait, Sheriff Turner," she said. He turned and looked at her. "I may not be here by next Friday and I found everything so confusing out there yesterday. I just thought reading your report would help me understand what had happened. I certainly don't mind reading the notes or rough draft or whatever you have." She smiled at him.

Obviously, that approach wouldn't work. Turner hadn't moved and he wasn't smiling. "Look, ma'am. I don't know what you're used to down there in Florida. Here we do crime reports once a week. Lots of weeks we don't have anything to write up. See, we don't have many criminals here. This is a nice small town. Most of our citizens are in church this morning." It was a pointed remark, pointed right at Emily. "We don't have many troublemakers. All we got is some boys that have a few too many beers and kick around their old ladies once in a while. As for Stella Love, she drank too much champagne and took a big step off a high spot." Sheriff Turner ran his hand over his thinning hair. "It's a damn shame, but we went to investigate an accident, not a murder."

"But Sheriff, surely you know that there were people at that party who might have had good reason for pushing Stella over that railing," Emily said, forgetting coquettishness. "I know John Hackett went upstairs before she fell and I saw Mrs. Hackett go upstairs, too."

"There're a lot of rooms upstairs in that house,

ma'am," the sheriff said, now obviously annoyed. "People have petty squabbles in this town from time to time, and there are rumors of one kind or another about most of the wealthy people in this town. But they don't go around pushing each other off balconies. You better go back to Florida for those stories. If you'll excuse me." He turned and walked into his office, closing the door behind him.

Emily was stunned. And furious. She hadn't so much expected professionalism, but she had assumed courtesy. There's probably a big box of donuts with his name on them in his office, she thought. The desk clerk was smiling at her as she turned to leave.

Outside, it was a beautiful day. Sunny, not yet hot, and the sky was as blue as the exterior of The Grand Palace, a huge multimillion-dollar theater that she'd read had been painted—at great expense—to match the sky so it wouldn't loom so large on the horizon.

Blow it off, she told herself. It's not your story, it's not your job. Just be grateful you'll soon be out of here.

She thought about the extra locks on the door of her apartment in Tampa, the parts of town she avoided after dark. The sheriff was probably right, but his attitude was so unnecessary. And what if he was wrong? What if the murderer who pushed Stella off the balcony was allowed to go unpunished because the sheriff refused to admit there was a killer in his fair town? Maybe the sheriff was protecting someone. In her more self-aware moments, Emily knew her cynicism about Ozark practices stemmed from the resentment she harbored toward her mother, but now that rancor was aimed at the law enforcement. As she backed out of the parking place, she looked at the two sheriff's department cars parked side by side. "Wonder how long it takes these good ol' boys to come out for an emergency call," she muttered. "Probably depends on whether or not it's coon-hunting night."

Emily stopped at a downtown convenience store and bought a can of caffeine-free Diet Pepsi—brown water, Jim called it. Then she turned left onto the state highway that led south to Blue Eye and to Arkansas beyond. She had nothing to do for the next few hours until Tony Orlando's matinee, so she pulled her favorite Jimmy Buffett tape out of her purse and slipped it into the car's player and headed south at a leisurely pace.

There was little traffic on the two-lane road. The sheriff was probably right about most people being in church this morning. Still, she glanced often into the rearview mirror to see if any cars were behind her. She wondered what John Hackett was doing right now—asking God to forgive him for pushing Stella over that balcony? Or maybe that's what Irene Hackett was mumbling under her breath as she paged through the hymnal.

At the sheriff's department, Ron Turner was on the phone.

"Irene?" he said. "Can you talk? I need to see you. Can you meet me for lunch at The Shack? Okay, see you at one."

Emily drove through a break in the steep rocky banks that had been cut to make way for the highway and made a conscious decision to stop thinking about yesterday's events and enjoy the sights. She slowed a little and looked out across the Ozark valley. It was a breathtaking view, especially for someone used to the flat, monotonous landscape of Florida.

For miles, Emily could see rolling green hills. Dark green areas of cedar stands contrasted with the brighter green of the oaks and sycamores, their shaggy gray bark flapping like banners from the tall straight trunks. Below to her right, snaking through a deep valley, a creek glistened. Above, Emily saw a hawk circling. Scattered here and there, she could just make out rooftops through the trees. She wondered where the roads were that led to the houses perched on steep hillsides. What a view to see each morning. Emily imagined sitting on a sunlit porch, sipping her coffee and looking out for miles. And nighttimes on that porch would be so quiet, with only the sound of whip-poorwills. Then she realized that in each of those visions, she was not alone. Jim poured her coffee in the first scene and sat beside her in a porch swing in the second.

Emily snapped out of her daydreams when she heard the pickup roaring up behind her. Instinctively, she touched the brake. She glanced in the rearview mirror just as the truck sped up to pass her. It didn't look like a safe place to pass on such a curve and Emily pulled over toward the shoulder to let the truck go by. As the truck pulled in front of her, a young man wearing a baseball cap backward leaned out the window. She couldn't hear what he yelled, but she watched the tobacco juice shoot in an arc from his pimply face and splatter on the pavement just beyond her car. Moments later, a white paper bag flew out the truck's window and remnants of a Burger King breakfast scattered on the roadside. "Lovely," Emily muttered. She contemplated only briefly trying to catch up with the truck to get its license number and report the boys for littering. Then she pictured Sheriff Turner's chubby face and dismissed the idea.

A few miles on, Emily saw the turnoff to Blue Eye. She turned onto the road and pulled over, debating the wisdom of a foray into the past. She had been so young when her parents took her to Florida, she was sure she wouldn't recognize anything about the town. She had seen a couple of black-and-white snapshots of the three of them standing in front of their small frame house, but surely it looked like all the other houses in such a small town. Maybe the hardware store was still there, but Emily wasn't sure she wanted to see it if it was. Then she realized she was probably never coming back here again, she could just as well cruise through and see what the burg looked like.

Blue Eye was twenty miles from the highway on a winding road, two lanes, no shoulders. She passed pastures where cows were already congregating under shade trees as the day warmed up. "Corporate meeting." Emily said to herself, then wondered if that was an expression her father had used. She couldn't remember. Emily knew the cows were dumb, but she liked their soft eyes, the placid way they ground their teeth, chewing an imaginary wad of gum. A couple of years ago, she had gone to the state fair in Tampa and had wandered through the cattle barns. It concerned her just a little that she didn't find the musty barn smells unpleasant. She recalled fishing with her father and wondered if she'd be able to spot the pond; there were a lot of ponds here, and the rolling pastures all looked pretty much alike.

Then there was a sign—Welcome to Blue Eye—Jesus Saves—and in smaller letters, From the Blue Eye First Church of Our Lord. Two miles on the Left. Emily smiled and glanced at herself in the rearview mirror, pushing a stray strand of hair into place. She reached into her purse for her pale pink lipstick and then stopped. "What are you doing, girl?" she asked herself. "It's not like you're going to Sunday dinner with the family."

As she got closer to the town, she passed several farmhouses, meager places where roofs had been patched with slabs of tin. Paint curled down from gutters and every car any relative had ever owned rested, rusting, in the side yards. As she slowed to heed the twenty-five-mile-per-hour speed-limit sign—imagining the sheriff's car lurking behind a billboard, waiting just for Emily—three dogs of no discernible breed sprang from the sagging porch of a tumbling house. They surrounded her car, following it, yapping and baying. Emily proceeded slowly until their territory ended and they headed back for their porch.

The only sign of small-town style Emily noticed were the mailboxes. In front of nearly every worn-out house, a mailbox perched atop a post anchored in a milkcan. Some of the cans had flowers painted on them, others were solid colors, but each was distinctive. Emily remembered the many crafts her mother had tried out over the years. She had made things out of popsicle sticks and clay that she baked in the oven. She had tried carving doll faces from apples, leaving them to dry and shrivel into grotesque caricatures. For a while she had taken up weaving place mats on a small loom she'd bought at a yard sale. Most of her projects turned into Christmas gifts for Emily. Most were packed in a box in Emily's spare closet. But Emily had kept the doll with the pink crocheted dress in her bathroom. It was a cover for a spare roll of toilet-paper and Emily had always considered it her mother's best work.

As Emily drove through town, she realized that the highway was the main street of Blue Eye. The entire downtown consisted of a dozen buildings, a small stone post office, a feed and grocery store, and a gas station. Nothing was open. Nothing looked as if it had been open for a long time. Some of the buildings had sheets of warped, graying plywood nailed haphazardly over what might have been a front window. Half a block farther down the highway, clumps of weeds grew through cracks in the blacktop paving around a building that had faded checked curtains in the windows. Marys—Best Eats in Town, a crooked sign in the window proclaimed. Bet this place was hopping last night, Emily thought. How utterly depressing. Why do people live here?

Emily swung her car into the restaurant's parking lot. Apparently she had already passed through the town. Nothing had looked familiar, and she felt disappointed.

Beyond the restaurant lay more road winding through pastures. As she was about to pull onto the highway to head back into the town, Emily saw three young boys, two about ten or twelve years old and one younger, maybe six or seven. They wore no shirts; bony shoulders protruded from their overalls. All three wore black-and-white hightop sneakers and they were running up the hill toward the nearest rundown house. Emily rolled down her car window, and she could hear them laughing and shouting to each other. They all carried fishing poles. The tallest boy held a stringer of catfish that he had to hold above his head so the half-dozen or so fish wouldn't drag on the ground.

"You have to tell Mamma I caught that big one," the smaller boy shouted to the others who were just ahead of him. "We will," the tallest returned. "You done good, Joshua," the other boy called. Looking back over his shoulder, he slowed to let the small boy catch up. Behind the boys, a dog resembling a beagle came up the hill, stopped to snuffle a bush, and lifted his leg to mark his place. The boys bounded across the front porch, slinging back the torn screen door, shouting to announce their return. Slowly the torn door closed and everything was quiet again in Blue Eye.

Emily had to let the tears come out. It hurt her eyes and throat too much to hold them back. A couple of good sobs was enough. She didn't know why she was crying. Those boys had been so happy, so proud, and she remembered the look on her father's face when she'd hauled in a foot-long catfish, unassisted, for the first time. The fish had flopped in the bottom of the boat, its long black fleshy whiskers splaying water. It was the ugliest fish Emily had ever seen, but, by God, she'd caught it. "And you did it all by yourself, sweet baby," her daddy had said. For dinner that night, her mother had fried up the day's catch. Filleted and cut into squares, dredged with cornmeal, spices and flour, and fried in hot lard, the chunks of fish all looked alike. But when her father carried the plateful to the table, he picked around with the fork and placed one chunk on each of the three plates. "This is the one you caught, sugar," he told Emily.

Emily sat and stared down the road through Blue Eye. Around some of the porches, clumps of marigolds and asters made bright patches like quilt pieces cut from favorite outgrown dresses. Behind one of the houses, she saw the straight rows of a garden, corn stalks, poles where beans and tomatoes climbed. To one side of the garden, a flurry of incoming and outgoing flights circled by a white beehive. The beagle lay on the nearby porch, head resting on crossed paws. She wondered which building had been Stone's Hardware, but she could find no giveaway trace of advertising on any of the buildings she could see. She watched the town for several minutes. Nothing moved except the honeybees. Emily blew her nose and dabbed her eyes, careful not to smear her mascara too much, then started the car. She drove slowly, looking at the porches of the small houses, hoping for something she might recognize. Each porch held at least one dog. They slept on wooden porch swings or chairs with the stuffing bulging from tears in upholstery. On one porch, a big hound stretched out on the bench seat from a pickup truck. None of them chased her car this time. Nearly every porch sported one or more hummingbird feeders, the red nectar beckoning in the sunlight. No familiar sights stirred Emily's memory and then she was through town again, back to the winding road and the quiet cows.

Emily felt dazed, moved, emotionally uncomfortable. She pushed the Buffett tape back into the player and turned up the volume. "Bring back the magic, don't make life so tragic . . . ," Buffett sang. "Oh, perfect," Emily said in disgust, and hit the fast-forward button, hoping for a happier song.

Halfway between Blue Eye and the highway, Emily saw a one-pump filling station. An old, dark green car parked by the gas pumps indicated that the place was open, and Emily pulled in. Her Pepsi was empty and she was suddenly thinking about cigarettes again, too. She walked inside the small store. From behind the counter, a plump grand-motherly looking woman smiled at Emily.

"How you doing today?" she asked, as though she thought maybe Emily hadn't been doing too well the day before.

"Fine," Emily said. She really didn't want to make small talk. She picked out a bottle of caffeine-free Coke from the small cooler and picked up a pack of Camel Lights from a display on the counter.

"Going to be a hot one again, looks like," the woman said as she rang up the total.

"Yes," Emily said, holding out three dollars.

"Need matches, honey?" the woman said.

"No. Thank you," Emily said and turned to go.

"You visiting kin in Blue Eye?" the woman asked.

Emily turned back and looked at her. The woman was smiling, leaning on the counter against her chubby arms. Just trying to make small talk in a small town that probably doesn't get many tourists. No harm in that.

"No," Emily said. "I'm visiting friends in Branson, but I used to live around here when I was a child, so I just wanted to drive out and look around."

"Oh, what was your family's name?" the woman asked, now perkier than ever. "Maybe I know'd them."

"I don't think so," Emily said. She was sorry she had let herself be drawn into the conversation. "We lived way out of town and were only here for a little while. Have a nice day now."

She rushed through the screen door, which closed with a bang behind her. She started the car before she even got the door closed and turned back onto the road.

"Not cool," Emily said aloud. "Definitely not cool. I could have been a little more pleasant." Emily turned up the Buffett tape, threw the unopened pack of cigarettes out the window, and watched the pack bounce into the weeds in the sideview mirror. When she saw the state highway signs a few miles later, Emily pulled over to the road's side and combed her hair. Looking in the rearview mirror, she touched up the smeared eyeliner and applied pale pink lipstick. She had just enough time to get to the show.

While Emily was reliving the past, Sheriff Turner was sitting in a back booth at The Shack cafe. Looking at his watch, Turner was only mildly annoyed that he was missing the Steelers–Broncos game. He'd have time to catch the last quarter.

It was exactly one o'clock when Irene Hackett came in. She was wearing blue jeans and a brown sweatshirt. She didn't look like a rich woman, nor did she look rested.

Ron Turner stood up. "Hello, Irene. You look like you didn't get much sleep last night," he said.

"You look like you didn't shave this morning," she replied without a smile. She slid into the booth across from him and looked at her watch, then glanced around the restaurant. Tourists filled a couple of tables, but the place was pretty quiet.

"I haven't got a lot of time," she told Turner. "What do you want?"

"I just wanted to talk to you without John leaning over your shoulder," he said. "That's all."

A waitress came over and they both ordered coffee. "Don't you want anything to eat?" Turner asked.

"I'm not very hungry today," Irene said. The waitress

left. Irene leaned back in the booth and rubbed her eyes. She folded her arms across her chest and looked at Turner.

"Why, Ron? Why did this have to happen? Things were just about manageable as it was, and now this," Irene said.

"You should have known something like this was going to happen sooner or later," Turner told her. "You can't go around playing with fire and not expect to get burned."

"I thought she was harmless," Irene said. "She would have just moved on like his other little friends did once they got what they wanted from us. Instead, she has to fall off the balcony, practically into the arms of an out-of-town reporter."

The waitress brought the coffee and a stainless-steel pitcher of milk. Irene stirred sugar and milk into her coffee.

"That's one of the reasons I had to see you," Turner said, taking a sip. "She came by to see me this morning, asking questions."

"I knew it," Irene said. She put her elbow on the table and rested her forehead in her hand. "It'll make great headlines. This town doesn't need that kind of publicity."

"Stella's falling off a balcony isn't much of a story," Turner said. "She told me she's just writing a travel article. Why are you so worried?"

Irene looked up at him. "I just don't want her trying to make more out of it than that. All she has to do is talk to about five people in this town to hear a lot of rumors about John and Stella. Don't you think she'll find that interesting?"

Turner slopped coffee onto the table and mopped it up with paper napkins from the dispenser on the table.

"She thinks someone pushed Stella off the balcony."

He didn't look at Irene. "She said you and John were both upstairs when Stella fell. She sounded like she was implying some connection."

He put down the clump of stained napkins and looked at Irene, who was staring back at him.

"What are you saying, Ron?" Irene said evenly.

"Nothing. I'm not saying anything. I'm just telling you what she said. Irene, you know I'd do anything for you. You know that. You know I'd rather have seen your husband lying on that slab than Stella, too."

He took a drink of coffee. "What do you want to do about this?" he asked.

She looked at him without a change in her expression. "What do you mean 'what do I want to do'? John and I were upstairs in the sitting room when we heard the waitress scream," she said. "I was telling him to start pushing coffee because everyone was getting too drunk. I didn't want those people there all night."

"If that's your story, Irene, there's nothing I can do except stamp this an accidental death. What if John didn't have an alibi for that time?" He watched her. "A woman doesn't have to testify against her husband," he said and hesitated for a moment. "But she can."

"Are you crazy?" Irene said, a little too loud. Then she lowered her voice again. "I don't know what you're suggesting, but I've told you what happened. That's all I've got to say about it. If Miss Reporter wants to write a scandal piece, there's nothing I can do about it. Why don't you turn your brilliant investigative powers in someone else's direction?" She wiped her mouth with a napkin. "Why don't you start looking for that guy who was stalking Stella down in Texas?"

Turner rubbed his hands across his unshaven face. "Why would I do that? He wasn't at the party, was he?"

"I don't even know what the guy looks like. But if you

64

want to make up unlikely scenarios you might as well think he walked in and killed Stella. We didn't exactly have the doors locked out there yesterday.''

"Is he in town? Did Stella say anything about the guy being here?'' Turner asked.

"No.'' Irene sounded impatient. "I'm not *saying* he was there. Tune in, Ron. I'm saying that you ought to think about pointing your finger somewhere else and not at John or me.''

"I'm not pointing fingers, Irene, and certainly not at you.'' He rubbed his forehead and looked at his watch. "I can see we're not communicating. But then we never did communicate too well, did we?''

"Maybe not. I have to go. I didn't tell John I was going out. He was busy doing something in the garage.'' Irene stood up and so did Turner. She looked at him.

"I know you're trying to help, Ron,'' she said. "But don't. Don't keep trying to get involved in my life. I'm doing just fine.''

"That's not how it looks to me,'' he said.

"It's none of your business,'' Irene snapped.

"I know,'' Turner said. "I'm sorry.''

As Irene walked out of the restaurant, a man who was coming in greeted her. She didn't speak to him. Turner sat back down in the booth. The waitress brought more coffee, but he waved her off and left two dollars on the table. As he walked back toward his office, Turner knew he was going to miss the whole ball game.

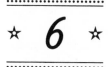

★ 6 ★

Tony Orlando's theater was a sparkling white concrete and glass structure highlighted by a forty-foot-high stained-glass yellow ribbon mounted over the entrance. And the theater even sat in a stand of oak trees. How appropriate, Emily thought as she drove up to it.

When Orlando had announced he was building a theater in Branson, he was among the first noncountry stars to arrive, and some predicted he would fail. Instead, according to the town's newspaper and the chamber of commerce director, Orlando's had become one of the most sought-after shows. He had the reputation of being sincere, out to give his audience their money's worth. Also, of critical importance, the man could still sing, people said. Although Emily couldn't have named a list of his hits, she was looking forward to the show.

In the spacious lobby, Emily wandered through the gift shop where rows of T-shirts were emblazoned with Tony's smiling face and costume jewelry beckoned from glass cases. All the clerks and attendants were friendly, smiling at Emily or greeting her as though they'd been expecting her visit. In Tampa, she would have been suspicious of such behavior, but after only a few days in the

Ozarks, she recognized the response as the naturally warm demeanor of the people.

Across the lobby, Emily caught sight of Monica Deal, dressed to the nines in a short denim affair with ruffles, fringe, and beadwork. Movie-star sunglasses added to Monica's glamorous look. Suddenly Emily felt plain, almost dowdy.

Maybe she'd have to go shopping for a Branson glitz dress for Friday's show. But Emily wasn't much of a shopper and hated the time it took from things she'd rather do. She wished that a lifetime's wardrobe for all occasions came with you at birth, like baby dolls with layettes in old Sears catalogs.

As she watched Monica schmoozing with people in the lobby, Emily's mind filled again with the image of a dead Stella Love, her blank eyes seeing only the spotlight from the sun. Emily's reporter instinct came to life and she casually sauntered across the lobby in Monica's direction.

"Hello, Miss Deal," Emily said, smiling at the blond woman. "Do you remember me? We met at the Hacketts' yesterday."

Monica froze for a moment, the careful composure sagging with her shoulders. Then it passed and the performer reappeared.

"Oh, of course," Monica crooned. "You're the reporter, aren't you? I'm so sorry, but I've forgotten your name."

"Emily Stone," Emily said. "I'm visiting from Tampa to do a travel piece. It was terrible about Stella, wasn't it? I haven't been able to think of anything else all day."

"Yes," Monica said, changing to a low voice. She adjusted her sunglasses. "It was a tragic loss to her friends and to the community. Have you seen Tony perform before?"

In a town whose motto was "If you don't hear a rumor

by eight A.M., make one up," Monica did not seem inclined to gossip about the tragic fate of Miss Love.

The crowd began to edge toward the theater's inner doors, and Emily moved along next to Monica.

"No, I haven't," Emily said. "I hear he does a great show."

"Well"—Monica smiled and leaned toward Emily as though a secret were about to emerge—"of course it's not as good as our show, but he's a good entertainer. I'm sure you'll enjoy it. I try to get around to everyone's show during the season. It's a form of professional courtesy here."

When they entered the theater, Monica glanced at her ticket and offered Emily what she had begun to realize was the standard farewell line in Branson.

"Come see us," Monica said. As she turned away to enter the dimly lit auditorium, she pulled off her sunglasses.

"Yes, I will," Emily called after her, realizing too late that it wasn't a salutation that needed a reply. Monica glanced back at her and Emily was shocked to see that her eyes were puffy and red. It could only have been the result of hard crying.

For the next hour, until the break for intermission, Emily was totally absorbed by Tony Orlando's performance. He was so dynamic in his connection with the audience that Emily felt he knew she was there and was singing the songs just for her. Not all the songs were familiar to Emily, but Orlando's rich voice and sense of showmanship entertained her completely. As the lights came up for intermission, Emily realized that she had indeed forgotten all about her problems, had even forgotten she was in the Ozarks, for that hour.

Back in the lobby, she again approached Monica, whose dark glasses were back in place. Monica stood near the front door, chatting with a cluster of tourists. At least

Emily assumed they were tourists since each of them had a camera dangling from their necks.

"Monica, you were right," Emily said. "It's a terrific show. His voice is even better than I remember it. And the crowd really seems to love him."

"I'm so glad you're enjoying it," Monica said. "The opinion of the press is still very important to us here in Branson. Who knows how many people in Florida will decide to come to Branson after you write your story? And I'm glad you're enjoying it because Tony and I go back a long way. I worked with him for a while in Vegas. Of course when you've been around as long as I have, you end up working with a lot of people."

"Monica, I'd like to talk to you about the changes you've seen in Branson in the last few years," Emily said. She also wanted to get Monica's reading on yesterday's events and find out what she was doing upstairs when Stella died, but caution kept her from mentioning that now. "Are you free for lunch tomorrow?'

Monica brightened considerably at this idea, Emily noticed.

"Yes, as a matter of fact, that would be just fine," Monica said as the lobby lights dimmed their warning of the end of intermission. "Why don't you meet me at McGuffey's at noon. Do you know where that is?"

"Yes," Emily said. "I'll look forward to it."

"Where are you staying?" Monica asked as they moved back toward the auditorium.

"I'm out at the Bitterroot Resort," Emily said. "Do you know where that is?"

"Sure," Monica said. "John Hackett built that place and ran it for a few years." Leaning close to Emily and touching her forearm, she said, "I wouldn't be surprised if there was a peephole in every bedroom. See you for lunch."

Monica was gone into the throng. Emily stared after her for a moment before the push of the crowd moved her along toward her seat.

The second half of the show was even better than the first. From a riser in the middle of the auditorium, Tony performed a medley of songs that had even Emily singing along. "Michael Row the Boat Ashore" had never sounded that good around campfires on the beach. A thousand people sang along in the dim light while a mirrored ball cast sparkles on the walls and ceiling. The riser where Tony stood was just one row from Emily's seat. She was close enough to see just how good-looking he still was at fifty, and Emily felt a surge of star-struck attraction and thought of the Neil Diamond poster she had kept folded in her nightstand when she was fourteen. Just the thought of ol' Neil in her nightstand used to put her to sleep with a smile on her face. Now she had that same feeling watching the sweat run down Orlando's face. This wasn't easy work, Emily could see. She wondered if it kept them young or killed them?

After the show, she strolled toward her car, dodging cars exiting the parking lot. It was after six o'clock and the cool of evening was setting in. Emily felt out of place as she made her way through the happy crowd, people laughing together, small groups and couples. She saw a man walking by himself and thought he must have been connected with the show, or a friend of Tony's. Then she realized the assumption she had made: surely he couldn't have been there by himself unless it had some connection with business. He was an attractive man who would have had his date or wife on his arm if it was just a pleasure outing. It was the kind of prejudice, deeply rooted, that confronted the "lonely guy" in Steve Martin's film, the guy on whom the spotlight shines when he enters a restaurant for a quiet dinner alone. Alone. Not a nice word, but not meaning the same as lonely. Or did it?

When she had almost reached her car, she passed a group of people reboarding their tour bus. There were more women in the group than men, but all of them were laughing and discussing the show. She overheard praises for the restaurant where they had eaten dinner, and excited talk about plans for the next day. They all wore matching T-shirts with the logo of the tour company. A woman teased one of the men and others joined in the good-natured jesting. It was obvious they were having a wonderful time. Emily considered sending her mother on one of those tours, and vowed to look into it when she got home.

Approaching her car, Emily went through the automatic safety checks she practiced in Florida: look under the car to see if some stupid crazed killer is lurking, ready to grab your ankles; as you unlock the door, check the backseat to make sure the same lunatic isn't lurking inside. It was a routine Jim encouraged. Sometimes she felt silly doing it, but not today. If there was a murderer in town, at least he wasn't in Emily's car.

With typical Ozark courtesy, Emily stopped to let a car pull out in front of her into the line waiting to leave the parking lot. It was Monica Deal. Monica didn't appear to recognize Emily. As they turned onto the highway, Emily wondered where Monica was going and decided to follow her. It'd be interesting to see what kind of a house Monica lived in. After a few blocks on the strip, Monica made a right turn into a residential section of poorly maintained frame houses mixed with trailers. No one was in sight along the narrow street. It wasn't what Emily had expected. Monica must not be making the kind of money Emily had guessed. Emily kept her distance, careful not to risk Monica spotting her. If she lived in a dump, Emily didn't want to embarrass her. Nor could she think of any reason to explain her presence in this neighborhood.

She noticed Monica slowing and pulled over behind a parked car. Halfway down the block, Monica turned into a gravel driveway and pulled her car behind a faded pink trailer. The yard was overgrown with bushes and the grass obviously hadn't been mowed for months. Emily got out of her car and slowly walked along the cracked sidewalk toward the trailer. If Monica happened to come out and catch her, Emily could simply say she needed to change the time of tomorrow's luncheon date and had decided to stop by instead of calling. As she neared the trailer, she glanced at the mailbox by the driveway. Her heart skipped a beat. ''S. Love,'' the mailbox read.

So it wasn't Monica's house. What was she doing here? Emily noticed a worn path in the grass that led toward the rear of the trailer. Checking to be certain there was no one watching her, she walked slowly along the path. The sun was down now and the light was beginning to fade, but no lamps shone from inside. I must be crazy to be doing this, Emily told herself as she pressed between two big lilac bushes. Now she was at the side of the trailer. She heard no sounds as she edged toward a window, careful to avoid a web where a large orange spider waited, and cautiously peeked inside. She was looking into a bedroom. On the wall opposite the window hung three identical posters of Lyle Malone and his backup singers. Taped between the posters were two press photos of Monica Deal. Then Monica walked into the bedroom. Emily ducked, then carefully peeked again. Monica had her back to the window. She was searching the drawers of a bureau, pulling out handfuls of clothes. Emily saw her remove one drawer, turn it over to look at the bottom, and then do the same with the next. From the lowest drawer, Monica withdrew a large brown envelope. She pulled out a sheaf of papers and stood up, looking through the contents. Then she put the papers back in the envelope and replaced the clothing in the bureau drawers. Next, Monica pulled her photographs off the walls and removed the posters. She left the room, carrying the envelope and the posters.

As Emily crouched in the bushes wondering what to do, she heard the back door close, then Monica's car start. She waited and saw Monica back out the driveway and head down the street. Emily made her way to the back door where a cracked cement block provided a step. She took a tissue from her pocket and put it over the metal doorknob, thinking how smart she was to consider fingerprints, and what a fool she was to go inside. The door opened easily. In the dim light, Emily could see the drainboard piled with dirty dishes. The kitchen, furnished with a small table and one chair, smelled like sour milk. The walls were bare. Just a quick look, Emily thought as she listened to her heart pounding. She walked quietly into the trailer's narrow living room. An old recliner faced a portable television that rested on the stained carpet. There was nothing else in the room. She crossed to the bedroom, where the twin bed was unmade, and the closet door was ajar and Emily pushed it open. Inside hung four floor-length beaded gowns. Two fancy western-style blouses hung beside them and a pair of jeans was draped over the closet rod. On the floor of the closet, a gray sweatsuit lay in a heap beside a pair of red and black cowboy boots. The sound of a car driving by gave Emily a sudden jolt. Quickly she left the trailer, using the tissue to close the door. She made sure no one was in sight before making the short walk back to her car.

Emily felt sick. So that was how the glamorous Stella Love had lived. All illusion. Monica had been her hero, her role model, and now Monica wanted to be sure no one knew that. Tired and confused, Emily drove straight to the Bitterroot, watching the traffic behind her all the way. She was relieved to see that Robert's truck was not in the driveway and that his cabin was dark. She thought of Fluffy, but no furball was in sight. She didn't even bother to call. She went inside, turned on the lights, and undressed, then forced herself to watch a movie on television. Later she called for the kitten, but there was no reply.

Emily made a few notes about Orlando's show and about Stella's barren home. Maybe she could work something into her story about the difficulty of rising to fame, paying your dues. It might be some small tribute to the dead woman. And she made notes on what she would ask Monica tomorrow at lunch: begin with questions about her career, what it had been like getting started, then try to lead Monica into talking about her relationship with Stella. Maybe she'd discover what Monica had taken from the trailer. It might be something she could tell Sheriff Know-It-All. Too tired even for a bath, Emily turned out the lights and slid between the sheets. As she drifted into sleep, she saw the proud boys with their fish, running into the house to their mother.

When Monica arrived back at her modest home on the north side of town, she saw the black pickup in her driveway. She could see Robert leaning against her front door. Monica got out of her car and walked up to him. They stood looking at each other. Finally, Robert cleared his throat.

"Can I come in and talk to you for a minute?"

Monica hesitated. "Why not?" She shrugged, unlocking the door. Inside, she kicked off her high heels. "You want some coffee?"

"I'd rather have a beer if you've got one," Robert said.

"Robert, I can't go through this again. Haven't we said everything there is to say?"

He slid his hands in his pockets and looked at his feet. "I guess I could use a drink, too," she said, sighing. Robert followed her into the kitchen, where she handed him a bottle of beer from the refrigerator, then poured an inch of bourbon into a glass for herself. They leaned against the kitchen counter. From the hallway, a grandfather clock chimed softly.

"Did you see what happened?" Robert finally asked.

"Yeah," Monica said. "She was drunk. She fell off the balcony. It was that fast. One minute she was being her normal nasty self, the next minute—" Her voice caught.

Robert reached over to where she leaned beside him and took her hand. They stood that way, both looking at the floor.

"I didn't even hear about it until this morning," Robert said. "I had breakfast at The Shack. Everyone was talking about how you and Irene should be so glad she's gone."

He put down his beer and turned to her. Monica came into his arms and they held each other. Monica's shoulders shook with her sobs. She pulled away and wiped her face with her hand. When she looked up at Robert, his face was wet, too.

"I loved her, you know," he said, also wiping his face. "You know I did, Monica. You know I never meant to hurt her."

She held him again. "I know, Robert, I know. I loved her, too."

Monica pushed him away and took a tissue from a box on the counter. They both sipped their drinks in the silence.

"I should have taken her back to Texas," Robert said.

"She wouldn't have gone. You know she wouldn't have gone with you, no matter what you said. I know how it feels to love something more than you love a man."

"Why couldn't she have been a little more patient?" He walked to the doorway and leaned there, his back to Monica. "She didn't have to take up with Hackett that way," he added, a hard edge in his voice.

"Well, you couldn't tell her that," Monica said. "God knows I tried to enough times. We both did. I told her it wasn't the right thing for her. But Stella couldn't see it. She couldn't see anything but the promise of glory in him."

"The son of a bitch," Robert said.

"He's a sick man, Robert. I hate his guts too, but you can't blame him for everything. Even Irene tried to tell Stella not to count on him for much."

"So now it's over. I can't believe she's gone." He turned in the doorway and looked at her. "What am I going to do now?"

Monica walked to him and laid her head against his chest. He put one arm around her shoulders and started to rest his cheek against her stiff blond hair, then leaned his head back against the door frame.

"You'll go on, baby, just like I will," Monica said. Neither of them moved.

"I'll probably go back to Austin," he said.

"You could stay in Branson," Monica said. "Maybe I could help you find a job. There might be something at the theater."

Robert patted her back and straightened up. Monica turned, got some more tissues and blew her nose.

"The guys at The Shack were speculating that someone . . . pushed her," Robert said. "The sheriff may come looking for me. Because of that trouble she made in Texas. You know I never did anything but try to talk sense to her."

"I know, Robert," Monica said. "Stella told me all about it, too. She said she knew you weren't trying to hurt her. She just didn't want you going into that club anymore. She was just being dramatic like she usually was. I don't think the sheriff will even think of you."

They listened to the clock ticking. "Where were you yesterday afternoon?" Monica asked.

Robert looked at her. "I was at Rustler's all afternoon. I shot pool and drank beer. Everyone saw me in there all day. Mike and Bernie and everyone can tell you."

"I didn't mean anything by it. What are you worried about the sheriff for if you've got an alibi?"

"I'm not worried. I just don't need any more hassles right now."

"Well, nobody but me even knows you knew Stella, do they?" Monica said.

"No. I only saw her twice since I came here, and I haven't really talked to anyone but you." He looked at her. "Who else could I have talked to?"

Monica sighed. "I don't know, Robert. If you're really worried about it, you can stay here if you want. Until you decide what to do. You can put your truck in my garage."

"No. I don't think I need to do that. I'll probably just go back south. Maybe I'll head out tomorrow." Robert went over to her and put his arms around her again. "I'm sorry. You know how sorry I am."

"I know," she murmured.

Robert leaned down and kissed her cheek. "I better go."

"Take care of yourself," Monica said. She walked with him to the front door. "Let me know where you are."

"I will," he said. "Good night."

Monica leaned against the door and watched him back out of the driveway. She stood there until his taillights faded. Then she went to her car and retrieved the crumpled posters and the papers. Back in the kitchen, she stuffed the posters into a garbage bag and poured herself another drink. She carried it into the living room, turned on the television, and walked over to a cabinet that held stereo components. From one of the drawers, Monica took out a small, gold-framed photo. It was a picture of a blond-headed little girl, about two years old. A tear fell on the glass. Monica wiped it off against her sleeve, put the picture back in the cabinet along with the envelope of papers, and quietly closed the drawer.

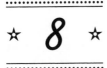

✶ 8 ✶

When Emily opened her
eyes, she was immediately angry at the shaft of sunlight
sneaking through the blinds and shut them again, trying
to make sure the dream she'd just had come back to her.
She rolled over and realized she missed the softness of
Shakespeare, her faithful twelve-year-old cat whose death
the year before she still mourned. Shakespeare had liked
to sleep with her, curled spoon-style against her. He had
always been equally unwilling to greet the dawn.

It often took Emily a few moments to remember
where she was and what day it was and what she had to do
that day. This day, she finally recalled, was Branson, Monday, lunch with Monica, but there was no rush so she
flicked on the TV to *Regis and Kathie Lee* and turned on her
left side, stretching her legs to relieve the crimp in her
lower back. She dozed for a luxurious hour.

Finally, she stretched and decided she would face the
day. She thought of Jim's morning energy. Some mornings his energy went into making love. Other mornings
she would wake to the sounds of him puttering in the
kitchen, the smell of coffee perking. Mornings with Jim
were always a surprise. Sometimes she would turn over and
ignore his presence, not wanting any words to be spoken

until she had actually put her feet on the floor. But the mornings he wasn't there, in contrast, seemed a little dull. She had often wondered if annoyance was better than emptiness.

Then she remembered the kitten. Donning her robe, she cautiously opened the cabin's door and looked out. Robert's black truck sat beside her rental car. It was absolutely quiet. The day was bright. Blue sky lit the lake and birds flew low across the silver water fishing without a cry or a license. She went back inside and set the coffee to brewing while she pulled on jeans and a blue T-shirt. After pouring black coffee into an Ozark Jubilee mug, she walked outside and sat in a wooden chair on the small porch that faced the lake. With a hum, a fishing boat went by, looking small and insignificant framed against the rocky bluff on the other side of the narrow cove occupied by the Bitterroot. Emily relaxed. She didn't even think for a few moments. She was almost lulled back to sleep by the rhythmic lap of the water against the shore and the fading drone of the motorboat, but roused herself to get ready for her day.

While she showered and dressed, Emily decided her first stop was going to be the sheriff's department. She couldn't believe he wasn't even willing to admit someone might have killed Stella Love. Maybe he'd be in a better frame of mind to talk to her today—or maybe she'd be better equipped to break through to him.

After a quick drive through McDonald's for a sausage biscuit, she headed downtown to the sheriff's department. The streets were crowded now with tourists bustling off for their scheduled recreation. The go-cart tracks buzzed at Emily as she passed. Ahead of her in the traffic, Friendly's Tour Bus belched great puffs of black smoke.

When she pulled into the parking lot beside the sheriff's department, she saw three marked cars. Picturing the whole force chowing down doughnuts together, she strode to the front door.

Inside, a different receptionist sat behind the window. He looked too young to be a deputy, but he wore the uniform. His face glistened with a ruddiness that looked as if he'd scrubbed it too hard this morning.

"May I help you?" he said with a friendly smile.

Emily pulled out her best "I like your looks" smile and said, "Yes, I'd like to see Sheriff Turner, please."

"I'll tell him you're here." The young man smiled, heading down the hallway. After a few steps, he returned. "Who should I say is here?"

"Tell him Emily Stone is back," she said, smiling, too. He turned and went to get the sheriff.

Emily ran her fingers through her hair, adjusted the collar of her white blazer, smoothed her short plaid skirt, and took a deep breath.

"Miz Stone?" Sheriff Turner said as he came up behind the glass window. He wore a crisply creased uniform and his shaven face looked almost as shiny as the receptionist's.

"Good morning, Sheriff," Emily said with a hearty smile. "I wanted to stop by and apologize for my attitude yesterday; I was just upset by everything that happened at the Hacketts'. Could I have a couple minutes to chat with you?"

Today her sweet approach seemed to work. It usually did. Emily had made it work with men and women, young and old, all stations in life. Just show a little vulnerability and you're in. Come across—even just a little—with a superior air and your chances of getting what you're after are nil.

"Sure," said the sheriff, wiping his chin with a white paper napkin, removing all signs of glazed doughnuts, no doubt. Getting slicked up for the assault.

"Come on back to my office," he offered, holding the door open for Emily.

The sheriff's desk was strewn with papers. A small photo of two girls of about eight and ten sat on one corner. Three faded prints of Rocky Mountain scenes hung on the wall facing his desk. The sheriff removed a stack of papers from the chair opposite his desk and added them to the accumulation, indicated the chair and asked Emily if she'd like to sit down.

"I guess we did get off on the wrong foot yesterday," Sheriff Turner said. "I get a little defensive sometimes because so many newcomers just want to run the place down. A lot of people are jealous of the success we're having here. I hear it all the time." He raised a mug. "Can I get you some coffee?"

"No, thank you, Sheriff. I just had some at McDonald's."

"You ought to try The Shack for breakfast while you're here," Turner said. "It's downtown on Commercial Street. Best home cooking in town. And it's the morning hangout for all the local politicians or the ones who think they're politicians. We pretty well solve the world's problems every morning from seven to eight."

He was much more pleasant-looking when he smiled.

"I'll have to try that," Emily said. "I've always heard that line about vacation food not having any calories, but I don't think that's true. I think I'd get hooked on funnel cakes if I stayed here."

She could have devoted another ten minutes to the friendly small talk, but decided she better not take the pandering too far.

"You know that I'm here to write a travel article about Branson, focusing on Friday's show. I'm not planning to write anything critical about Branson, and I've found it a very interesting place so far. It's also not my job to write any sort of news story about Stella Love's accident." She put no special emphasis on the last word. "But when I was at the Hacketts' party, I overheard some things that made me curious. I probably got the wrong idea about some things and I thought you'd be the one to set me straight."

Turner was taking another sip of coffee, so she couldn't see if his expression changed.

"I have the impression that Stella Love wasn't exactly loved by everyone."

The sheriff's chair creaked as he shifted his weight. He reached for some papers on his desk and began to straighten them.

"Ma'am, I must hear more of the rumors in this town than anyone," Turner finally said. He leaned back in his chair. "I guess I've heard them all about Stella and Hackett, and it's apparent that you've heard some too, but that doesn't mean he pushed her off the balcony, you see what I mean? He says he was with Irene when the commotion happened. Irene also said they were together. I have no reason to doubt that. Do you?" He looked steadily at Emily.

Well, here it was. She'd put herself in a position where the sheriff was interviewing her about the situation, and Emily wasn't ready to tell him the truth. She didn't want to say she was upstairs with her ear against the wall listening to John Hackett carrying on with Stella Love nor did she want to tell him about going through Stella's house.

"I did hear the rumor of an affair between John and Stella," Emily said, watching for a reaction. "I also heard that John was impotent. Maybe Stella found out and was blackmailing him."

The sheriff didn't move. "They both have alibis for the time Stella died."

"It was my impression that John was upstairs and Irene was out at the stables when it happened."

"Did you see them?"

"Not exactly. That's what Irene told me after it happened. Didn't she tell you that?"

The sheriff looked at her steadily. "Everyone was in a state of shock. Maybe Irene was a little confused when she talked to you. And maybe she didn't want to talk to a reporter right at that time, either."

"Well, a lot of people could have seen Stella go upstairs. Someone else could have followed her."

Sheriff Turner shuffled the papers on his desk. The silence was uncomfortable.

He pulled a sheet of thin fax paper from among the mess on the desk. He looked at her again. "I don't know why I'm going to tell you this. You have no official capacity here, but maybe it'll satisfy you that the people in our department are fully capable of running an investigation. We are looking into the possibility that someone might have done what you just suggested. It seems Stella might have had someone, well, stalking her, as they say these days. One of my deputies tells me that Stella told some folks several weeks ago that she was worried an old boyfriend from Texas might follow her up here and give her some trouble, not that John would have been likely to let that happen."

The sheriff tapped the fax paper. "I called up the police department in Stella's hometown yesterday afternoon and today they sent us a report on this fellow. Seems she'd gotten a restraining order issued after he'd harassed her. Apparently she'd told him to get lost and he'd come in and caused trouble at the club where she was working. He didn't assault her, just made threatening noises, I gather. We've got his description and the make of his pickup. We're keeping an eye out for him up here and the police down there are trying to locate him. But it's pretty farfetched to think that he could have come into the Hacketts' home, pushed Stella off the balcony and left without anyone seeing him. And no one remembers seeing any strangers at the party."

Emily thought of the open, unattended front door, of the crowds milling throughout the house. She recalled the silent upstairs rooms, closed bedroom doors. If she had lurked undetected in one of them, someone else could have done the same. But she couldn't tell that to the sheriff.

"So does that provide you any reassurance that we're not totally incompetent?" the sheriff asked.

"I never underestimated your capabilities, Sheriff Turner," Emily lied. "I just wanted to be sure you had all the information you might need and offer my help."

"Well, did you see any young men lurking around the room Stella was in?" Turner asked. He looked at the fax sheet. This guy's twenty-eight years old, six feet one, slim with brown hair and blue eyes. He drives a 1979 black Ford pickup licensed in Texas."

"No, Sheriff. I didn't notice anyone upstairs with Stella. But there were a lot of people there and most of them were strangers to me."

"If this guy's up here, we'll run across him," the sheriff said, laying the fax back down among the jumble of papers. He opened a desk drawer and pulled out a pack of cigarettes. "Mind if I smoke?"

"Go right ahead. There must be a lot of men up here from Texas these days with all the jobs available around here. Probably a lot of them drive pickups." This is pointless, Emily thought. All I'm doing is annoying him again.

"Well, sure there are. But you'd be amazed how often we catch someone who's come here to hide out." He leaned back in his chair and took a drag on the cigarette.

Emily didn't say a word. She felt a story coming on.

"Guys on the run come up here to the Ozarks because they think there aren't many cops and that they can get lost back in these hills. Maybe find a little shack to hole up in somewhere and lie low. What they don't realize is that neighbors around here have their own security network." Turner fiddled with a pencil, drumming it against the chair's arm.

"Within two days of a newcomer moving in, everyone for five miles knows all about that person's business, and if they don't, that raises their suspicions. That's usually when I start hearing about it." He puffed on the cigarette. The smell was making Emily's mouth water.

"In the past couple of years," the sheriff went on, "I've caught a fugitive wanted on suspicion of murder, a bank robber, and a guy wanted for making methamphetamine. And they had all rented the same little trailer about six miles south of here. What they didn't know is that the old boy who owns the dump is a better spy than anyone the FBI's got. And the guy wanted for drugs was mixing up a batch of the stuff the morning I walked in."

The sheriff laughed at his own story. Emily laughed a little, too. After a polite pause, Emily said, "Well, do you have the license number of that black pickup? Maybe I can get in on the security network, too."

The sheriff fumbled again for the fax. "LPJ 392," he said. "Texas plate. Keep an eye out for it. In the meantime, just relax and enjoy your stay in town." He stood up. "Is there anything else I can do for you today, ma'am?"

Emily stood up, too. "No, not a thing. Thank you for taking the time to see me." She shook hands with him and turned to leave. She could feel him watching her as she walked out. At the door, she turned back. "What was the man's name who was stalking her?"

Turner looked at the fax. "Robert Smith. Sounds like a phoney name, doesn't it?"

"Thanks again. Have a good day."

When she had gone, Turner closed his office door and dialed a phone number.

"Irene? It's Ron. Can you talk? I wanted you to know our favorite reporter was just here. More questions." Turner paused. "She said she'd heard a rumor that John was having troubles of a sexual nature. Impotence, she said. She thought maybe Stella was blackmailing him over it."

He listened. "Okay, okay, Irene. I'm just worried about you. Your life is your own business as you've made very clear to me. I'll be talking to you."

Back in her car, Emily pulled out a notebook and wrote down the license-plate number she'd memorized. Surely, she thought, in a town with hundreds of construction workers, stagehands, and waiters, the cowboy I kissed last night couldn't be a stalker who pushed Stella Love to her death. The fact that he drove a black truck and said he was from Texas must not be at all unusual here. And the initials have to be coincidence.

But she did resolve to check the license plate of Robert Simmon's truck next time she saw it.

Emily looked at her watch. It was eleven-thirty. Nearly time to meet Monica for lunch. And besides, she reasoned, if Robert had killed Stella, why would he still be hanging around? Why would he have made a date for dinner tonight with her? This was none of her business. "Just stop thinking about it and do your job."

McGuffey's was crowded. Men and women in suits filled the booths and tables, along with a smattering of tourists, but Emily realized this was primarily a local crowd. As she stood inside the entrance, the hostess came up to her.

"How many today?" the pretty young woman asked.

Emily thought about looking behind her and snapping, "Well, how many of me do you see?" Instead she said, "I'm meeting someone here. I'll just look and see if she's here yet."

"Are you meeting Monica?" the hostess asked.

"Yes," Emily said, surprised that she'd forgotten again the small-town ways.

"She's already here. She told me to watch for you. Just follow me." It occurred to Emily to wonder how Monica Deal had described Emily to the hostess—"Watch for a mousy little reporter."

The hostess led Emily through the busy restaurant to a dimly lit dining room in the back where she saw Monica sitting in a booth across the room. She was looking into a compact mirror and touching up her tomato-red lipstick. Emily recognized Andy Williams at another table, noticing a lot more wrinkles in his face than the billboards and advertising photographs showed. That must explain the lighting back here, Emily thought. A favor for the stars. As she walked past his table, he looked up at her.

"Hello, Mr. Williams," Emily said.

"Hello," he said, and smiled at her. She could see that most of the wrinkles in his tanned face were involved with smiling. It gave his face a warm, friendly look and she understood then why his fans were so devoted to him.

"Hi, Monica," Emily said, as she approached the table. "How are you?"

Monica looked better than she had the night before. She wasn't wearing the dark glasses and the redness in her eyes was barely noticeable. A considerable amount of makeup hid any dark circles that might have shown. Every blond hair was in place and Emily wondered if it was a wig. A red satin blouse with shiny beadwork on the collar and cuffs topped off a long denim skirt and red boots. For a moment, Emily felt plain and underdressed again.

"Well, I'm just fine," Monica drawled. "Have you had a nice morning?"

"A lazy morning," Emily said. "I slept late and had coffee out on the porch. Very relaxing."

The waitress brought them menus. Monica didn't

open hers. "You must not get much chance to relax during the months you're putting on the show, do you?" Emily asked.

"Really, I don't," said Monica, stirring a packet of NutraSweet into her iced tea. "People think we're just here raking in the money and lolling around when we're not onstage. But it's not that way. Six days a week I do the morning show, then sometimes I catch a nap, but several times a week we have rehearsals for changes we make from time to time during the season. Plus I do lots of charity work, fund-raisers and appearances. You wouldn't believe the requests we get for our time. And then there's the show every night, and we all stay to sign autographs. Most nights I don't get home until midnight, so it's really grueling. But it's worth every minute of the work when I'm out on that stage."

The waitress returned. "Are you having the usual today?" she asked Monica. Monica nodded. "Try the Thai chicken salad," she advised Emily. "It's delicious and low-fat, too." Emily followed her advice.

"Singing onstage is what I've dreamed of my whole life, from the time I was a child," Monica continued. "My grandmother used to sing to me, and she loved the old music from the 1930s, so I grew up listening to Bob Wills and the Weavers and the Carter Family. When I was little, I used to use an old wooden spoon as my microphone. Being a singer was all I've ever wanted to do, and like most of us, I'd do anything to stay in the business."

Just then an older couple walked toward them and stopped a few feet from the table. The woman was clutching a pen and an autograph book and both of them were beaming at Monica.

"Hello," Monica said.

"Hello, Miss Deal," the woman said. "I'm so sorry to interrupt your lunch, but we had to leave right after your show last night to get back on the bus and we couldn't stay to get your autograph, but we just love you so much. Would you mind very much signing my book? We're Millie and Richard, from Indiana. Would you mind?"

"Of course not," Monica said, reaching for the book. When she finished, the couple thanked her as though she'd just signed a check to pay off their mortgage and bustled away, reading what she'd written.

The waitress brought the salads, heaping portions that looked good enough to make Emily realize she was hungry again. I have to stop eating so much, she thought. But at least I'm not smoking.

"Doesn't that just get to be a pain in the neck?" Emily asked, nodding in the direction of the autograph seekers. "Don't you ever want to tell them to go away?"

Monica put down her fork and patted the napkin gently against her red lips. "No, never," she said. Emily thought her cheeks got a little more pink beneath the makeup.

"Those are my customers. They're the ones who pay my bills. I owe every good thing in my life to them. My fans and that spotlight are what keep me young, keep me getting up every morning. Every night, there's a different audience to please and so it's a new challenge all the time."

Monica sipped her tea and cleared her throat. "The best part is watching someone in the front row who obviously doesn't want to be there. You can see them. They sit with their arms crossed and look at their watch a lot; usually it's some husband whose wife has dragged them in to see Lyle. I look right at him when I'm singing, you know, make eye contact in a way that makes him think I've got a little crush on him? To see that man smiling by the end of the night, clapping along, maybe giving his wife a little nudge while I'm singing the "Tennessee Waltz" because it roused some memory in him of the time he was courting her—that's my reward. It's better than money, better than sex, better than anything I've ever known."

Emily was so stunned by the vehemence of Monica's monologue that she had forgotten to eat. "There must be some downside to what you do, Monica. The way you work can't leave you much time for your family, does it?"

Monica took a bite of a piece of raw broccoli and didn't answer while she chewed. She swallowed and sighed, and Emily saw her get a little older right before her eyes. The little wrinkle lines seemed to seep through the makeup and Emily thought Monica's lower lip quivered just a little.

"I have no family," Monica said, her chin rising slightly with defiance. "I had a daughter, but I haven't seen her for a very long time. I was very young and I put my career first. That was all I ever thought about. When you're driven, when you want that spotlight shining on you more than you want to eat, when singing to an audience is the only thing, and I mean the *only* thing, that makes you feel good and human and happy, you do whatever it takes."

Monica's fist was clenched so tight her knuckles glistened white. "I gave up everything for my career. I got ahead any way I could. And I have no regrets."

A convincing performance, Emily thought. She knew from her years of doing interviews that when you'd hit an emotional chord in someone it was the best time to keep asking questions. Get someone on a tender subject and you never knew what kind of surprising answer you might hear.

"Tell me the truth, Monica," Emily said softly, leaning forward over the table. "Don't you worry about aging? It must be a concern that you might someday be replaced by a younger singer. Are women like Stella Love much of a threat?"

Emily knew she'd hit a target. Monica put down her

fork and reached for another packet of sweetener. Her sleeve caught her iced-tea spoon and it fell to the floor. She nearly knocked over the glass of tea, and Emily was almost sorry she'd mentioned Stella.

"I warned Stella," Monica said in a low voice that trembled with emotion. She stirred her tea vigorously with her fork. "I pleaded with her to forget about the business, find a job where she didn't have to get up every morning wondering if she'd grown a new wrinkle in the night. I told her to go home, get married, and have a family so she'd have someone who cared about her when she was too old to attract a man anymore."

Monica's eyes narrowed. "But then she met John Hackett. I told her what a snake he is. He's the most ruthless son of a bitch in the world. That's not to go in print, you understand." She stopped and looked at Emily.

"Of course not, Monica," Emily assured her. "We're just visiting. Go on."

Monica dabbed at her lips again. "I told Stella she was nothing to him. She was just another young woman that he could suck the blood out of to stay alive. He sucks them dry and then throws them away. I've seen him do it." More dabbing. "I told her John would destroy her. He wasn't trying to make her a star. He was throwing tidbits her way so she'd follow him like a mouse to the trap. I told her the first time she didn't want to play his game anymore, he'd put her on the trash pile with the other ones. But she wouldn't listen to me. And now it's too late."

Monica held her napkin against her lips and closed her eyes.

Eager to keep Monica talking, Emily pressed on.

"Did you know the sheriff thinks someone was stalking Stella?" she asked. "Some guy from Texas."

Monica put down the napkin and picked up her purse. She fumbled inside, looking down into the purse as if searching for something. "No, I didn't know that," she said without looking up.

One more, Emily thought. "I overheard someone last night say they thought John pushed Stella off that balcony. Do you think he could have done something like that?" Emily watched for a reaction. "I think he was upstairs then. Did you see him when you were up there?"

Monica snapped shut her purse and glanced at her watch, then straightened up to look at Emily. Her stage smile was perfectly in place and she looked as though she hadn't heard the last question.

"Gosh, I didn't realize how I'd been prattling on," Monica said, patting her stiff hair. "It's nearly one and I'm supposed to be at the theater at one for rehearsal. Do you mind awfully if we finish this conversation at another time? I really have to dash."

"No, of course not," Emily said, disappointed by her lack of success.

Monica gathered her large purse and a scarf, and offered Emily her hand. "I'll be around all week," Emily said. "You know I'm staying out at the Bitterroot, so if you have time for lunch again, please give me a call. I'd love to continue our conversation."

"I will," Monica assured her hurriedly. "Thanks so much. Come see us."

Emily stood there and watched Monica sail through the dining room, handing out her smile as if it were a carefully wrapped Christmas gift.

Emily sat back down. She took another bite of her salad. Weird, she thought. Does she want me to think she thinks Hackett killed Stella? What was that all about? Stella might have been the biggest career threat Monica's ever had. Why would she seem so upset over her death? I've just seen some kind of an act, but I don't know which play I'm watching. I wonder which bedroom Miss Deal was in? God,

I'm glad this isn't a story I have to write. A hundred to one Monica won't be calling me to have lunch again.

After Emily paid her bill, she decided to go back to the resort and get some work done. The town's main strip was jammed with cars. Traffic crept along, so Emily did what everyone else was doing and looked at the array of entertainment possibilities. One of the most unusual was an ancient-looking wax museum, housed in several interconnected single-wide mobile homes. They had all been painted a gaudy yellow, with brightly painted illustrations of the wonders awaiting inside. "See the Corpses of Leading Mafia Bosses," one sign read. " 'The Last Supper'—Life-size." "Marilyn Monroe and Elvis—Together at Last." Emily couldn't help but laugh. That I'd like to see, if I have time later this week, she thought. Next door was an elaborate minigolf course where a chubby gray-haired woman was carefully aiming a putt toward a windmill whose arms turned slowly. Two other women with the same short curly hairdos stood beside her laughing and pointing out how she should aim the shot. Back in Iowa or wherever these women lived, they probably hadn't been on a minigolf course in forty years.

The strip was lined with go-cart tracks, ice-cream shops, stores hawking T-shirts and swimsuits, a store that advertised 1,000 Souvenirs, Nothing over $1, and, of course, funnel-cake stands. She had lied to the sheriff. Emily hadn't tried a funnel cake since she'd been in Branson. In fact, she'd never heard of them until she came here. So she pulled into one of the stands and paid three dollars for something the size of a pie plate. As she watched, thin donut batter was poured into a funnel-shaped nozzle and dribbled in an irregular pattern into a vat of hot grease. When it was fried to a golden brown, the funnel cake was dredged in powdered sugar. The result, Emily found after breaking off a chunk to eat, was very sweet, heavy and greasy. But it grew on her and she ate more chunks of it as she got back out into the traffic, dribbling powdered sugar on the floorboards.

Throngs of people strolled along the sidewalks, mostly groups of older women, occasionally a family or a couple holding hands. After more than half an hour of edging along at five or ten miles an hour, Emily was glad to turn off onto the road leading to the lake resort. It was surprising how concentrated the developed areas were and how quickly the scene changed once she left the strip behind. Now Emily was in the country again, driving past small farmhouses set on the rolling hills. She passed the place where she might have met her death the night before if things had gone a little differently. Today, in the late-afternoon sun, nothing seemed threatening.

Maybe I'll take a swim when I get to the cabin, she thought. I sure hope this place doesn't grow too fast. It's really beautiful here. I should bring Jim before it changes too much.

When Emily pulled up to her cabin, hers was the only vehicle around. That was a relief. And Fluffy was sitting on her stoop, licking a paw.

As she opened the door, the kitten ran right in, and she was glad she had thought to stop at a convenience store for several cans of tuna. Fluffy purred as she wolfed down the treat.

Emily sat at the kitchen table and sorted through the piles of show brochures she had collected, making notes on some of the attractions she wanted to mention in her article. Fluffy curled up on one of the chairs and went to sleep, as if she owned the place. The little cabin seemed more like home somehow with another life inside.

Emily had a hard time concentrating on her work. She paced and looked out the window toward Robert's cabin. She examined the few outfits of clothes hanging in her closet and wished she had brought more variety. She was to meet Robert at six at Rocky's. She should have brought her old pair of jeans, the ones that fit so well and seemed right for dinner in Branson with a cowboy. She remembered a soft tan suede jacket she'd seen in a shop window downtown.

At four o'clock, Emily gave up on work and took a shower. She used the blow dryer on her hair, bending at the waist and fluffing her hair so it would look fuller and some of the natural curl would come out. She dressed in dark brown cotton slacks and a pale brown silk blouse. Everything she'd brought seemed too businesslike. At four-thirty, Emily carried the kitten outside, gave it a farewell snuggle, and headed downtown to shop, telling herself it wouldn't hurt just to take a quick look.

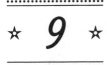

9

Downtown, Emily had to circle the block twice before finding a parking place near the Dressed to Kill shop. The clothes in the window display glittered in a shaft of late-afternoon sun. Mannequins wore long and short beaded gowns with elbow-length gloves. The price tag dangling from the floor-length lavender dress read $350, a fraction of what a dress like that would cost in Tampa, Emily thought. Inside, a woman who might have been in her thirties greeted Emily and asked if she was looking for anything special. The woman wore skin-tight jeans and a peasant blouse. A fairly tame outfit for Branson. Then she noticed the four-inch-long rhinestone earrings that dangled on her bare shoulders.

"I'd just like to look around," Emily said.

"Well then, you just go right ahead, dear," said the woman. "I'll be in the back, so you just sing out if you need any help. Try on whatever you like. The dressing rooms are right there."

The clerk pointed toward a sign that read Fitting Rooms and moved away through the narrow aisle.

Emily picked out a couple pairs of jeans, the least gaudy ones on the rack. One had a pattern of rhinestones across the hips. The other had fringe down each side. She found a pale blue cotton blouse, long-sleeved, but with the shoulders cut out. And she picked out a short denim dress with a fairly tasteful pattern of pearl beadwork on the breastpockets and collar.

She hung the clothing in a dressing room and went back to take one more look to see if there was anything else she wanted to try on. Glancing around to see if anyone was watching her, she looked through the rack of long beaded dresses, just for fun. The clerk was nowhere in sight. At the front of the store, a few tourists clucked over the fashions they were finding. Like a mischievous child, Emily picked a bright red sequined dress priced at $400 and carried it into the dressing room. She tried it on first.

The dress must have weighed ten pounds, Emily realized as she pulled it on. The low-cut front had a built-in push-up bra arrangement that flattered Emily's small breasts. She held her breath as she zipped the dress, then stood back to look. She felt like a fairy princess, like a little girl playing dress up. It was a beautiful dress and Emily felt beautiful wearing it, turning this way and that in front of the mirror. Finally, she talked herself into being practical and unzipped the gown. I have no place to go where I could wear this. I can't spend $400 just to play dress-up. What would Jim think about taking me to Marina Jacks wearing this? She smiled. He'd love it. He'd tell me I was his princess.

She hung up the heavy gown and tried on the other items. The denim dress fit like a glove and flattered her figure. So did the jeans and blouse. She was pleased; often it was a trial to find clothes for her short frame. When she emerged from the dressing room, she laid the jeans and blouse and the denim dress on the counter by the cash register and hung up the red dress on the rack. Then she went to the side of the store where boots were displayed. As though Lady Luck just wanted her to spend some money to support Branson's economy, she found a pair of brown leather boots in her size. The boots had scroll patterns of black stitching on the toes and up the sides. The only concession to flashiness was the silver toe caps. Emily pulled them on and found, to her surprise, that they were comfortable and didn't pinch her toes.

So she carried the boots up to the counter, too. Then she picked out a pair of dangly silver earrings. She walked back to the rack where the red dress hung and looked at it again, then turned away. She decided she'd better call the clerk before she changed her mind.

"Well, you've got a whole new outfit here, don't you?" The clerk beamed. "Got a special date coming up?"

"Kind of," Emily said. These people sure aren't shy about asking questions, she thought. "Could you cut off the tags? I'd like to wear this."

Emily changed in the dressing room, stuffing her old clothes into the shopping bag. Then she had to find the clerk again to help her pick out a belt for the jeans. At the clerk's insistence, Emily bought a silver concha belt, but drew the line when a cowboy hat was recommended to complete the ensemble. She felt awkward enough with her shoulders bare and rhinestones glittering from her hips.

"You look great," the clerk assured her. "I hope that cowboy knows what a lucky man he is."

Emily started at this, but then realized the clerk was just making conversation. Out she went into the sunlight. As she strolled along the street toward her car, Emily looked into shop windows. She could have been examining the displays, but she was really looking at her own reflection. Four storefronts later, Emily decided she liked what she saw. The look was blatantly sexy, but in a kind of homespun way. It just seemed natural in this town.

When Emily walked into Rocky's, she felt as if everyone turned to look at her. In fact, they did, but Emily realized it had nothing to do with how she was dressed. It was just the small-town curiosity and openness at work. She wasn't even overdressed in comparison to some of the other women in the lounge.

Emily sat at a table toward the rear of the bar. Robert wasn't there yet. She had circled the parking lot looking for his truck, remembering the license-plate number the sheriff had given her, but there were no black pickups. It wasn't quite six yet. Emily ordered a gin and tonic.

As she took the first sip, a man who had been sitting at the bar approached her table. Emily braced herself for trouble. The man appeared to be in his early fifties. He wore a dark brown Western-cut suit with a bolo tie and black boots. He also wore a big smile.

"Excuse me, ma'am. I couldn't help but notice you when you came in, and I wondered if you might let me join you for a drink. A pretty lady like yourself shouldn't be all alone," he said.

"Thank you, no," Emily said, smiling back at him. "I'm meeting someone here in a few minutes."

"Well, you can't blame a man for trying, now can you? I'll just excuse myself, and I hope I haven't offended you, ma'am," he said and returned to his seat at the bar.

That was easy, Emily thought. And fairly pleasant, too. She remembered men at dance bars in Tampa who hadn't been so polite, who approached her with silly lines like "I think I know you" or "Come here often?" At least this guy had been straightforward and polite.

By the time it was 6:20 and Robert hadn't arrived, Emily was beginning to fume. She felt a little foolish about the $200 she'd just spent on the new outfit, but rationalized that she'd done it to please herself, not Robert. By six-thirty, Emily had debated whether to stay and have dinner, risking Robert coming in late and seeing that she had continued to dutifully wait for him, or to leave and find another place to eat. Just as she decided to stay, both be-

100

cause it was the most convenient thing to do and because she would then discover if Robert was just late or he had stood her up, Lyle Malone walked in.

Lyle wore the same outfit he'd had on when she met him at the Hacketts' party: rhinestone-studded overalls, white shirt, black string tie. He held a black cowboy hat in his hand as he made his way through the tables, greeting people and stopping to talk along the way. He seemed to know everyone in the place and seemed glad to see them all. She could hear his deep laugh resonate across the room. As he worked his way back to the bar, he saw Emily and headed in her direction.

"Well, hello there, Miz Stone," he said, holding out his beefy hand. "How are you getting along?"

"I'm just fine, Mr. Malone. Nice to see you," Emily replied. She felt self-conscious again about her bare shoulders.

"Would you let an old man join you for a drink?" Lyle asked. "I'd be pleased to sit with the prettiest gal in the place."

"Sure," Emily said, pulling out the chair beside her. "I'd be pleased to have you join me. I was supposed to meet someone here for dinner, but I don't think he's going to show up."

"Well, now that's the way it is with these young fellows," Lyle said. "It's hard to find one you can depend on anymore."

Lyle deposited his ample frame into the chair and put his hat on another chair. From his breast pocket, he pulled out a bandana and mopped his face. "I've been a-running and gunning today, trying to line up everything for Friday's show."

"Don't you have a show to do tonight?"

"No, my theater's dark on Mondays. Even God rested one day a week," he said, chuckling.

Lyle ordered a bourbon and Coke and when the waitress left, he looked at Emily. "Looks to me like you've done some shopping in Branson. You look as pretty as a bird dog."

Emily laughed. "That's a compliment I've not received before," she told him. "I feel a little silly in this outfit, but I felt silly in the clothes I'd brought from home, too. Am I overdressed?"

"Not at all, darlin'. That's one of the joys of Branson. People come here on vacation and they feel free to do things they wouldn't consider at home. They can wear what they fancy, eat whatever they want because everybody knows vacation food's got no calories," he joked. "An old man can pinch his wife's bottom maybe for the first time in twenty years. And when they're all crowded up to get back on their tour bus, he might even pinch someone else's bottom." Lyle laughed at his own idea.

"What you're supposed to do here is have fun, relax, get away from all the things you're going to have to think of again when you get back home," he said.

"I'm here to work, but the spirit seems to have rubbed off on me," Emily said.

"Well, good," Lyle said. He looked at her and his expression became serious. "I'm a pretty good judge of character most of the time and you look like you could do with a little fun, Miz Stone."

Just for a mment, Emily could have sworn Lyle was seriously flirting with her. And, just for a moment, Emily thought that lying beside the big man with his meaty arms wrapped around her might not feel too bad.

"Please," she said. "Call me Emily."

"Thank you, Emily. I'm Lyle. So what should we eat tonight, Emily?" he said, picking up the menu. "Remember, no calories."

They ordered three dinners. Lyle couldn't decide between the spaghetti and meatballs and the lasagna, so he

102

told the waitress to bring both. Emily chose the linguine with red clam sauce. Lyle also ordered garlic bread, toasted ravioli appetizers, and salads. It was easy to see how Lyle kept his overalls filled out.

The food arrived quickly, and while they ate, they talked about country music. Lyle was a storehouse of country-music history and the role the Ozarks played in its development. It made perfect sense that Branson would become the live-entertainment capital, he said. It had a lot to do with the people who settled in the hills before the dams were built that formed Table Rock and Taneycomo lakes.

"While most everyone was going west, there were some folks that didn't want to fall in with the rest of them. This part of the state was settled by Scotch-Irish stock," Lyle said. "They were tough individuals, a cantankerous lot. They ditched the wagon trains and stayed away from the built-up communities because they didn't want anyone telling them how they had to live. Down here in the hills, they could get away from civilization and do what they wanted. It's the same kind of spirit you feel in this town today. It's the reason we can wear whatever strikes our mood and be proud of it."

Emily could see Lyle had strong feelings about the subject and she didn't interrupt. After breakfast, lunch, and a funnel cake, she wasn't too hungry, but the food was so good. And, besides, she couldn't smoke.

"And there's another side to those first settlers, too," Lyle went on. "I hope to hell we're not losing it with so many newcomers flocking here to get in on the abundance we're enjoying right now. The people that settled in these rocky hills were hunters for the most part. They'd scrape out a little plot for a corn patch and hunt the deer and bear, and that was their diet, corn for flour and maybe a little moonshine if they had enough corn left over, plenty of game on the table, and then they could take it easy." Lyle shoveled in a big bite of spaghetti. "Those people valued their time. They wanted leisure more than they wanted fancy houses or St. Louis clothes. And by God, they had time to sing. They had time of a summer evening to sit on their stoops and sing about their feelings, just like country folks were doing in other mountains around this land."

Lyle called to the waitress and told her to bring two glasses and a carafe of red wine. Then he leaned over close to her and said softly, "Miss Emily, if you go sit by Table Rock Lake on a night when the moon's full, I promise you'll hear a fiddle tune, slow and sad, rising up from that water." Lyle took a big bite of lasagna and winked at her.

Emily was impressed. She hadn't given much thought to the history of what seemed to her to be just a culturally deprived area. Through the rest of the meal, Lyle turned the conversation to Emily, asking about her family, her job, the kind of life she led in Florida.

It surprised Emily how she opened up to the man. She told him about her father, her fond memories of fishing with him as a child, and his death.

"He kind of abandoned you just when you needed him most, didn't he?" Lyle said.

Here was a man in overalls who said between bites of pasta what it had taken her Tampa psychologist six weeks to determine, Emily thought.

"I could have saved about six hundred dollars on a shrink, Lyle, if I'd talked to you first," Emily said. Lyle patted her hand and gave it a squeeze.

In return, Lyle told Emily about the pain of losing his wife of thirty-two years to breast cancer. In the three years since she'd died, Lyle said he'd felt lost and confused. And especially sorry that they'd never had children.

"It's not that other people noticed much," he explained. "I kept on with the show and did those things that we have to, but going back at night to that home she'd made for me and not having her there to share it, well, it's still the hardest thing I do every day. It's like I lost my right arm. Life just doesn't have as much meaning with her gone. I believe we humans were meant to live in pairs with each of the two doing what they do best and giving that to the other, watching each other's backs and keeping the wolves at bay. We all have a lot of love to give. The hard part is finding someone who won't charge us too much for it." He chuckled at his own gem of wisdom.

Lyle poured a little more Chianti into their glasses.

"It's too bad it can't work out that way for more people," Emily said. "I hardly know anyone who's happily married or satisfied with the relationships they have. Look at the Hacketts. They seem to have everything you could want, but I sure had the impression there was a lot of trouble in that paradise."

Immediately, Emily regretted mentioning the Hacketts. Lyle's expression hardened and he put down his fork and took a drink of the wine.

"Miss Emily, sometimes people turn out to be fools. We start looking at sixty, and seventy's right at our heels, and we try to hang on to something we can't have. John Hackett's a sick man, has been for a long time, and Irene's not much better in her own way. Hackett's sick because he knows there's nothing useful he's ever going to do in his life. Irene's probably been sorry for twenty years that she didn't marry Ron Turner. She was just out of high school, working as a secretary at the bank when John Hackett came to town. She'd dated Turner all through high school and they were engaged to be married. She was a beautiful young woman, and I figured she had good sense. But Hackett swept her off her feet, impressed her with his money, and she broke off her engagement and married

John. Now Ron Turner's a respected man in town, got a nice wife and two kids, and all Irene's got is a big empty house and a son-of-a-bitch husband, excuse my language." Lyle wiped his beard with his napkin. "It was a sad day for a lot of people when John Hackett came to town."

"Especially for Stella, I guess," Emily said. "Do you think she fell over that railing?"

"I don't think about it," Lyle said with a little too much vehemence. "There are things we shouldn't think about, answers we can never know. I suggest you don't trouble yourself over the affairs in that household or you may find yourself with more mud on your shoes than you can clean with a stick."

Lyle reached out and took Emily's hand in his. He raised it to his lips and kissed the back of her hand. "You're a nice young woman, Emily," Lyle said quietly, looking into Emily's eyes. "I'm telling you as the best friend you'll ever have in this town, just leave it alone." He kept looking at her for a moment. Then he patted her hand and pushed back his chair. From his overalls pocket, Lyle pulled out a roll of bills and peeled off a fifty, which he slipped under the wine glass.

"I've got to take my leave now," he said. "An old man like me needs his beauty sleep and there are probably a dozen young boys in this place waiting for me to get out of their way. Thank you for your company tonight, my dear. Come see us."

Emily sat watching him go and felt sad. She kicked herself for bringing up the Hacketts. Things were going so well and she'd been enjoying Lyle's company. Remember not to mention the Hacketts to anyone unless you want the lunch or dinner to end abruptly, Emily told herself.

She noticed several heads turn her way after Lyle left, so before anyone could approach her, she gathered her purse and made her way out to the parking lot. She considered stopping at the Copper Penny's lounge to hear the blues band again, but she was tired and felt a bit drained. She was disappointed that Robert hadn't shown up, but glad too in a way: if a man was unreliable it was better to find out as soon as possible.

And she certainly had enjoyed her conversation with Lyle. She had found him attractive in a very physical way even though he was more than old enough to be her father. Driving toward the Bitterroot, Emily speculated about just how far she would have gone in relating to Lyle if the circumstances had come to that. She pictured being in his embrace, feeling his big, warm body pressed against her. If the way he embraced her hand was any indication, she guessed he'd be a good kisser. Driving along the country road—watching in her rearview mirror for headlights—Emily allowed herself to imagine Lyle's whispered endearments as his big hands explored her breasts. Emily was quite wrapped up in the fantasy until she got to the part when she unfastened the buckles of his overalls. She couldn't get past that.

"She reached up and slipped the fasteners of his overalls so the straps fell back off his broad shoulders," Emily said aloud. She laughed and shook her head. It doesn't work. What a goof I am, making up sex fantasies about my newfound friend, the country star. I certainly hope my thoughts don't magically get broadcast through the Table Rock Lake ghost network.

Back at her cabin, Emily called for the kitten, who came eagerly running from a nearby clump of bushes. No lights came from the cabin next door. No black pickup. She considered leaving Robert an angry note, but decided it would be futile and ill-advised.

Emily carried the kitten inside, got the half-empty can of tuna out of the refrigerator, and set it on the floor. As the kitten lapped it up, Emily got ready for bed and bragged aloud about her evening.

"Like my new look, Fluffy?" Emily said. "I'm into the

country-girl look here, glitter in all the right places. And I got me a country star of my own, Fluff. Next thing you know, I'll be singing by his side every night."

Emily went to sleep with the kitten curled up near her shoulder.

Four miles away, on the other side of Table Rock Lake, Lyle Malone leaned back in a recliner in the living room of his spacious lakefront home. He wore pale blue cotton pajamas and house slippers. The flickering light in the room came from the television set where a videotape of Lyle's show panned the audience as they laughed, applauded. A tear ran down his furrowed face.

10

On Tuesday afternoon, the backstage area of Lyle Malone's Ozark Theater looked like an upended beehive. People scurried around, shouting orders to each other, as they got the theater ready for Friday's Hot Country show. Multicolored spotlights flashed on and off, and the sound of hammering punctuated the strains of a Lyle Malone recording. Walking through the open stage door, Emily was nearly trampled by a woman carrying an armload of costumes wrapped with billowy plastic into the theater.

No one watched the entrance door or challenged Emily's business backstage, so she stayed close to the wall, out of the flow of traffic and moved toward the stage wings where several men were busy unpacking and putting together video-camera equipment. Snaking lines of cables crisscrossed the floor, some taped in place with paths of duct tape. A dozen people worked onstage and another dozen scampered around catwalks and perches above the stage. The costume woman came back with a second load over one arm pulling a rack of glittering dresses. A long-haired blonde wearing a black leotard and tights walked across the stage and squatted to talk to a man taping down cables.

Emily thought she'd never seen anyone so thin. If she turns sideways, we'll lose her.

On the far side of the stage she saw Lyle engaged in conversation with several stagehands. Emily walked down a long hall running the length of the broad stage. The first door was labeled Green Room. Inside, a six-year-old boy holding a can of Mountain Dew sat on a couch watching the television across the room. The room was lavishly appointed with dark green leather couches and tartan plaid chairs. Dark green carpeting muffled the sound of her footsteps as she wandered around the room looking at the framed photographs of Lyle and other stars: Mickey Gilley, Glen Campbell, and Lyle together holding golf clubs; Lyle shaking hands with President George Bush. There were framed pieces of sheet music—songs Lyle had written, Emily noticed—and centered beneath the beam of a track light were two gold records in frames.

The little boy never looked up from his television program, even when the costume woman poked her head in the door.

"You being a good boy, Thomas?" she asked. She smiled at Emily. "He's too sick for school today, and I couldn't get a babysitter," she explained. "Mom'll be through soon and we'll stop at Burger King on the way home." She was gone again.

Emily moved on down the hallway. Next was a closed door displaying a brass star and the words "Lyle Malone." Farther along, the doors were open to four more dressing rooms. Mirrors topped by rows of bulb lights ran on three sides of each room, white Formica countertops held a hodgepodge of makeup jars and boxes of Kleenex. In one of the rooms, two blond wigs sat on mannequin heads. One looked just like Monica Deal's hair, Emily noticed. Linking each of the dressing rooms were three shower rooms with bathrooms. They all boasted toilets and urinals, so Emily couldn't discern any gender distinctions. Must get cozy back here, she thought.

The long hall ended at the far side of the stage. Lyle was nowhere in sight now, so Emily walked onto the stage toward the center where four steps led down to the auditorium. At center stage she stopped and looked out at the view the performers had every night. The three-thousand-seat auditorium loomed like the inside of a dark cavern. She couldn't see the farthest reaches of the room; the balcony seats receded into blackness. She hadn't been on a stage since the small role she'd had in her high school's senior play. She had played the family's maid in *Cheaper by the Dozen*.

This is the only time I'll ever be onstage in Branson, she mused. As she stood there wondering how the applause sounded from the stage, she was shooed out of the way by a stagehand who told her they were about to lower a fly. She went down the steps and turned to see a huge American flag descend from above the stage. Several of the shows climaxed with a patriotic number, flags waving, a sure way to get a standing ovation.

Emily walked back a few rows and took a seat in the empty auditorium to watch the bustle onstage. Just as she noticed a sweet, heavy scent in the air, a deep, rasping voice behind her said, "Well, look who we have here."

She whirled in her seat and saw that John Hackett had come in from the rear of the auditorium without a sound. He sat in the row in back of her and leaned forward, resting his folded arms on the chair to her right. His yellow teeth glowed with the reflected stage lights and she smelled an unpleasant mix of tobacco smoke and English Leather.

"Hello, Mr. Hackett," Emily said. "You startled me. You shouldn't sneak up on a girl like that."

"Sorry," he said, pulling a pack of cigarettes out of

the pocket of his tweed jacket. He took one out and put it between his lips, then offered the pack to Emily.

"No, thank you. I've quit."

"Hard to imagine a pretty lady like you being a quitter," he said as he lit the cigarette. "So, have you been keeping busy around our little town?"

"Yes," Emily said. "I wanted to watch the rehearsals this afternoon, but it looks like it'll be a while before things are in order here."

"Oh, you'd be surprised how quickly this all comes together. These people are the best in the business. When I knew I'd be producing this show, I called in the best people from all over the country. And believe me, I know them all. Most of them owe me favors, too." He began telling her names and résumé credentials of stagehands, light and sound technicians, and costume designers. None of it meant anything to Emily, and she wished he'd go away. Then she thought of the technique she'd used lately that seemed to end conversations.

"How's your wife?" Emily asked. "She seemed pretty upset over the accident last weekend."

"Well, honey, my wife's a strong little woman when she wants to be," Hackett said. "She wasn't always that way, but I've encouraged her to have a mind of her own. I'm a nineties man, you know?" He flicked cigarette ash on the carpeting. "I think it's fine for a woman to work, if that's what she wants to do. Makes her feel important, you know? Like yourself." He grinned and leaned closer to her. "I'll bet you're real good at what you do, isn't that right?" he asked in a low voice.

Emily maneuvered in her chair so that her purse fell to the floor. When she leaned to pick it up, she moved as far away from the leering figure of John Hackett as she could.

"I hear you're getting around pretty good," Hackett continued. "Dinner with our star last night?"

112

"How'd you hear that?" Emily asked. "And it wasn't a date or anything. We both happened to be eating at Rocky's last night and sat together." She stopped, wondering why she felt she needed to offer any explanations to this unpleasant man.

"Oh, you know how small-town gossips start a story out of nothing, just two friends having dinner and pretty soon it's a full-blown love affair according to the rumor mill. Too many people don't know how to mind their own business. Sometimes it can be a hurtful thing. Gets way out of hand." Hackett dropped his cigarette butt onto the carpeted floor and ground it out with his foot.

"You better watch that Malone, though," he continued. "That sweet old guy's a real lady-killer, if you know what I mean."

"What sort of hogwash are you telling her?" Lyle said as he walked up behind Hackett. "Aren't you supposed to be meeting with the sound man right now?"

"I'm about to do that, Lyle," Hackett said, getting to his feet. "You take care of your business and I'll take care of mine. I just saw our newspaperwoman sitting here and thought I'd better fill her in on who she's been dating lately. Enjoy your dinner at Rocky's last night?" Hackett looked at Lyle with what Emily could only characterize as a slimy smile.

Emily thought Lyle looked as if he'd like to take a swing at Hackett.

"You got to watch this old bear," Hackett told Emily as he moved past Lyle toward the aisle. "When you've been hibernating too long, you get pretty hungry, don't you, Lyle? You'd have liked to taste some of Stella's honey, but you didn't get to it fast enough, did you, boy?" He patted a tight-lipped Lyle on the belly.

"Why don't you just shut up and get the hell out of here?" Lyle said between clenched teeth.

"Talk nice to me, Lyle," Hackett said. "Listen, missy,

I'm having a little shindig on my houseboat tomorrow, just a few of my close friends. Lyle'll be there, won't you, Lyle, and Irene, of course. The boat's quite a rig, isn't it, Lyle? Got some real nice equipment on board. It's nothing fancy, just an eighty-footer, but we'll make sure you're real comfortable tomorrow. Come down to the marina at two o'clock. You can't miss the *Good Times*. She's the biggest one down there. And"—he paused—"I hope you brought your Florida bikini."

Hackett turned and headed up the aisle into the darkness, coughing and laughing. Lyle mopped his face with the bandana.

"What a creep," Emily burst out. "Why do you put up with him? And why does Irene put up with him?"

Lyle took some time folding his handkerchief and replacing it in his breast pocket. "I don't know the answer to that, Miss Emily. Just because a person's older than God doesn't mean he's got all the answers. Come on and let me show you around this theater," he said.

By the end of the afternoon, Emily knew a lot more about audio feeds and digital cameras than she'd ever hoped to know. She'd toured the production truck parked behind the theater that would transmit the television picture of the awards show to affiliates all over the country. She'd spent twenty minutes in Lyle's dressing room while he showed her his collection of autographed baseballs and bats, including his pride and joy, a Louisville Slugger signed by Mickey Mantle. "Baseball's the only thing more American than country music," he told her, while she thought of how much Jim would love to see these things.

Next Lyle had hauled her around introducing her to everyone backstage, some of them twice. He was proud of his $12 million theater, from its state-of-the-art soundboards right down to the newest kind of popcorn machines.

"When people come to my show, they pay money they've been saving up for their one-and-only vacation and I owe them the best—right down to fresh popcorn," Lyle said.

When Lyle had run out of things to show Emily, she told him she had to go and thanked him for the tour.

"How about we go catch a bite to eat before I have to come back and get ready for tonight's show?" he asked with a big smile. "Since we've already got the rumor mill running, we might as well take the fun with the blame."

Emily thought seriously of accepting. What would be the harm? But for some reason that she didn't understand, she found herself politely declining.

"Thank you, Lyle. I'd love to, but I really have to catch up on my writing. I keep forgetting that I'm not on vacation," she said. She reached to shake his hand and to her delight, he held it and kissed it solemnly.

"Will I see you tomorrow on the *Good Times?*" he asked.

"Sure," Emily said. "It sounds like fun. I'll just make sure I don't lean against any railings."

She regretted the flippant remark as soon as the words came out, but Lyle seemed not to notice and they said goodbye.

Back at the cabin, Emily was bored. Fluffy was nowhere in sight, she really didn't feel like writing a draft of her story, but she didn't feel like going out, either. She wished she had brought home something to eat. She looked at the cans of tuna, but that wasn't appealing. Not that missing a meal would hurt her after all she'd eaten yesterday. She thought of taking a swim, but instead she lay down on the couch and turned on the television. To the drone of a 1950s movie, Emily fell asleep.

She woke with a start to the sound of a car door slamming outside her cabin, then the slam of the screen door on Robert's cabin. It was dark and the television was the only light in her cabin. Emily walked to the window and slowly pulled the curtain open just a crack. There was no black pickup. Instead, a nondescript silver car was parked beside hers.

Robert must have left, she thought, feeling a twinge of disappointment, but mainly relief. If he's guilty of anything, it's in Turner's hands now. Glad I didn't go check out his "hot spot" the other night.

Since she no longer had to worry about running into Robert Simmons, Emily decided she'd take a stroll down to the lake. Maybe she'd see Fluffy. She pulled on a lightweight jogging suit and sneakers and went out. It was a warm evening, but not muggy. The sky was clear of any mist and the reflection of the waning moon looked like silvery ribbons laid across the rippled surface of the lake. Emily felt herself relax.

From the lake's edge, she looked back at the cabins huddled beneath the surrounding cedar trees. No lights showed from her cabin. From the cabin next door, a bluish light seeped through the curtained windows. As she walked slowly back toward the cabins, she noticed what looked like a small reflector low on the wall of the lighted cabin and wondered idly what it was. As she got closer, Emily thought it looked like a hole in the wall where the light from inside shone through. She remembered Monica's comment about peepholes.

Surely not. Emily shook her head. Surely it's just a knothole in the wood. She wasn't close enough to see exactly what it was, but she didn't want to walk right up to the cabin, either. Someone inside might see her. Then she saw Fluffy sitting by the wall, close to where the tiny beam of light emerged, and a devious idea came to her mind.

"Here, Fluffy," she called quietly as she approached the kitten and the hole in the wall. "Here, kitty." Fluffy came toward her a step and she scooped up the cat, lean-

116

ing down with her eye ever so close to the hole. At first she was just looking at the hole itself. It definitely wasn't a knothole. It was a neatly drilled hole in the exterior siding. Then she stepped just a little closer, clutching the soft kitten, and put her nose against the rough wood of the outer wall. She could see the inside of the cabin's bedroom. The bed was in full view. I'll be damned, she thought. This is too weird.

She glanced around over her shoulder as Fluffy meowed. Scratching the kitten's ears to quiet her, Emily took another look through the hole. The bedroom light was on, but no one was in the room. Then she saw shadows of movement from the other room and heard what sounded like the oven door being closed. The next second, Robert Simmons walked into the bedroom.

She could see him clearly, and she stood like a statue, afraid any movement might give her away. She saw Robert take a suitcase from the closet and flop it onto the bed. He took a handful of clothing out of one of the bureau drawers and tossed it into the open suitcase. Then he crossed again to the closet and added several items of clothing still on hangers to the suitcase. When Robert moved into the bathroom and turned on the light, Emily slowly and quietly backed away from the wall toward the lake, crouched over, still clutching the kitten. As soon as she was a respectable distance from his cabin, Emily stood upright and made a beeline for her own door. Before she could reach it, the porch light of Robert's cabin came on and he strode out the door.

"Hey, there you are," he called. "Good timing. I was on my way over to see if you've had dinner yet. I've got a pizza warming in the oven that I hoped you'd help me eat," he said with a broad smile.

Emily stammered. "Oh, hi. No, I've already eaten, I, uh, I'm really not hungry—"

"Well, then keep me company while I eat," Robert

117

offered, turning back to his cabin. "I'll grab a couple of brews and the pizza and be right over."

Emily carried Fluffy into her cabin and dumped the cat onto the couch. She quickly turned on all the lights and was wondering what to do when Robert came through the door carrying a pizza box and beer bottles, which he deposited on the table.

"You'll have one piece with me, won't you?" he called. Emily came out of the bedroom. Robert was already seated at the table, pizza box open, untwisting the cap of the second beer.

"Listen, I'm really sorry I couldn't make it down to Rocky's last night," he said. "I got tied up checking out a job prospect and by the time I got away you'd have been long gone. I'm sorry. Will you forgive me?" He flashed her a charming smile coupled with a pleading little-boy look. "Please, darlin'?" he said.

"It's no big deal." Emily shrugged, while she asked herself why she didn't just tell him to get out.

"Where's your truck?" she asked. Immediately, she wanted to bite her tongue.

"The damn carburetor screwed up again, so I rented that piece of junk yesterday," Robert said around a mouthful of pizza. "The garage said they should have mine ready by noon tomorrow."

He tore off a piece of pizza and held it out to Emily. "Here, try it. It's pretty good."

Emily decided she had to play it cool, so she sat down across from him at the table and took a slice. While they ate, Robert talked nonstop about the money-making scheme he and another guy were cooking up. It had to do with selling time-share property and Emily could tell by the way Robert tried to explain the deal that he didn't understand it, either.

Robert went from one subject to another as he had

118

the other night, barely giving Emily a chance to say a word, and it occurred to her that he'd probably had a few beers before he'd got back to the cabin. Some of his words were slurred just a little, and not only was he on a talking jag, he was repeating himself, telling the same stories she'd heard at their last dinner together. Robert finished his beer and headed to Emily's fridge.

"Got any beer in here?" he asked as he opened the door. Without waiting for an answer or an offer, he helped himself to a bottle. "Ready?" he asked Emily.

"No, thanks." Before she could say more, Robert launched into a story about his carburetor troubles with the old truck. She would have found him completely boring except that he peppered his stories with enough colorful phrases to keep her entertained.

"You know, my grandmother always told me, if something has tires or tits, it's going to mean trouble." Robert laughed at this himself. "It's always proved to be true for me."

Within a few minutes, Robert got another beer and brought one for Emily, too. This is the last one, she thought. Then I'll tell him to go.

Robert started on another story about his grandmother, and Emily's mind wandered. She had never known her grandparents. Her father's parents had stayed in Oklahoma when he had moved on to Missouri. Her mother's parents had both died before Emily was born. She had always regretted that she didn't come from a big Walton type of family. Suddenly she tuned in to Robert.

". . . could be such a bitch. Not that she didn't really mean to be. Nobody ever gave her anything, you know? Her mother ran off and left her, the people who adopted her treated her like dirt, so she just grew up thinking she had to be tough enough to take care of herself." Robert ran his hand over his beard.

"But she used men, used me, used everyone. She knew how to get what she wanted, too." Robert definitely sounded drunk now. And angry. He was jabbing his finger at a pile of pizza crumbs on the table.

"She'd put on those short skirts and low-cut blouses and she could get whoever she wanted. I was nothing to her. Just a little step on the ladder. It didn't matter that I loved her. Maybe it would have someday, but love's a matter of timing. It's got to be the right time of the moon and stars for both people or it turns sour. She wasn't going to change. I told her it'd get her in trouble, but she wouldn't listen to me, didn't want to hear it." Robert stopped to take a swig from his beer bottle.

"Your grandmother?" Emily said.

Robert looked at her. "My grandmother?"

"Are you talking about your grandmother?"

Robert put down the beer and leaned over the table toward Emily. "No, darlin'," he said. "I'm not talking about my grandmother. I'm talking about the love of my life, present company excepted."

He reached out for her hand, but Emily quickly stood up and carried her plate to the sink. Fluffy ran toward her and got between her feet, causing Emily to tip the plate and spill the pizza crust and crumbs on the floor. She leaned down to pick up the mess.

"I'm talking about a beautiful little girl with a voice like Emmy Lou Harris and not a brain in her blond head," Robert was saying. He leaned both elbows on the table and bowed his head, resting his forehead against the top of the beer bottle. "She knocked 'em out in Texas. She woulda made it. I told her not to go."

He looked at Emily squatting on the floor. "Just once in a while," he said slowly, "just once in a goddamn while, it wouldn't hurt you women to listen to us, you know?"

Emily stood up. "Who are you talking about?" she said quietly.

120

"I'm talking about the dead, darlin'," he said. He held up his beer bottle. "To the beautiful departed Stella." He took a drink, drained the bottle, and stood up unsteadily to go to the fridge. Emily knew there was one more bottle in there. Emily reached for the broom that leaned in the corner of the kitchen. Here was someone ready to talk about Stella Love, but what was he going to say? What if he talked about pushing her off that balcony? Emily got the broom. She thought about getting the gun, but realized that if Robert were dangerous, the last thing she'd want to do would be to let him know there was a gun handy. I don't think he's dangerous, Emily told herself. He just said he loved her.

"I met her last week," Emily said. She had a tight grip on the broom handle. Robert weaved back to the table and sat down. He opened the bottle and tried to spin the cap on the table. "She was beautiful," Emily said.

"Yeah," he said, and took a drink. "But she didn't know it. She didn't know how good she was. I told her, but it didn't make any difference. She should have just stayed home. We would have been happy." Robert's voice broke a little and he stared at the floor. When he looked up at Emily, she thought his eyes looked moist.

"Did you have a fight with her out here last Friday?" Emily asked. "The first night I arrived?"

Robert looked at her blankly.

"Remember?" Emily said. "You asked me if I'd seen what kind of car it was. We heard it racing out of here."

"No," Robert said. "She wasn't out here, at least not to see me. I didn't see that car, either. That's why I asked you if you had. It kind of sounded like her voice. But I couldn't tell. I'd spent so much time dreaming about her coming back, telling me she was sorry and wanted to mend things. I wouldn't have known her voice if I'd heard it that night."

Robert slapped the knee of his tight jeans. Emily

jumped. "I don't know why I'm unloading this on you," he said. "It's not polite to talk about a woman to another woman. It's just got me caught in a thicket, I guess. Forgive me, baby?"

That did it. Emily could see "trouble" stamped on his forehead. She'd already got too close to this man, and she could see that he wanted a port in a storm right now. Even if he wasn't a killer, Emily wanted him to leave. One way or another, he was bound to be bad news.

Still holding the broom, she took the pizza box off the table and set it on the kitchen counter. "Listen, Robert, I've got a full day tomorrow and I really need to get some sleep. Why don't we get together later this week, okay?"

"Well, now I've gone and made you mad, haven't I, honey?" He grinned and stood up, and Emily gripped the broom with both hands. "I'm sorry," he said, stretching. He cracked his knuckles. "I guess I've kind of had it for the night, too. How about tomorrow night? I'll meet you at Rocky's and then we'll go try that two-step later. How about it, sugar?"

"Sure," Emily said. "That sounds great. Thanks for the pizza."

Robert stood there looking at her as if he wasn't sure he should believe her. Then he slipped his fingers into the front pockets of his tight jeans and turned for the door. He pulled the door open, then turned back and walked toward Emily. He reached out and touched her cheek gently with the back of his hand. She tensed every muscle, ready to shove the broom handle into his face. "I'm sorry," he said again. "I hope I didn't offend you. You're a pretty woman."

"I'm fine, Robert," Emily said. "I'll see you tomorrow." She let go of the broom with one hand long enough to give him a soft punch to the front of his shoulder, like the male-bonding gestures she'd so often seen Jim make with his softball buddies. "Get some sleep."

He headed for the door. "G'night, ma'am," he mumbled and closed the door behind him.

Emily waited a couple of seconds, then hurried to the door and turned the lock quietly. She leaned against the door and breathed a sigh. She heard his door slam. "Geeeez," Emily said softly. That could have been bad. He's a mess. How stupid to have let him in here.

Fluffy came through the bedroom door walking sideways, rubbing her muzzle against the doorjamb. Emily picked her up and snuggled her against her cheek. "We got lucky tonight," she said. "He left."

Emily walked through the cabin making sure all the curtains were tightly closed. She peeked out and saw no lights coming from Robert's cabin. Then she went into the bedroom and started looking for signs of a peephole. She shone her flashlight behind the bed and the dresser and in all the corners. She had nearly decided that the hole in Robert's cabin was some kind of anomaly when she glanced at the plastic plate through which the television cable entered the room. Just above the cable's hole, another hole was barely noticeable. But there it was. Emily turned off the light in the bedroom and got down on her knees and put her eye to the hole. First she just saw blackness. Then she could make out the trunk of a tree.

This *is* the twilight zone, Emily thought. She stuffed a tissue into the hole. So there, John Hackett. Try to see through that. Emily spent several minutes more looking closely for any other holes, hiding places for cameras or anything else that seemed odd, but she found nothing. And she was tired, worn out from the tensions of the day.

She undressed and put on Jim's T-shirt. A calming

conversation with him would be nice, but she couldn't tell him what she'd been doing this evening, so she gave up on the idea of calling, picked up Fluffy, and crawled between the soft sheets, hoping she'd dream about palm trees and not cedar trees. Nothing woke Emily that night. Not even Robert's car pulling away from the cabin before daylight.

★ 11 ★

Houseboat party, Emily thought moments after she woke up. Then she thought of Robert next door. She got up and peeked through the curtains. His car was gone. Emily got back into bed where Fluffy was still curled up. It made the cabin feel so homey. Emily thought motels with resident pets you can rent would be a good idea. It might reduce stress on traveling businessmen if there was a beagle in every room.

Emily got up and put on coffee. She wondered if she should call Sheriff Turner and tell him about Robert. She really didn't even know if Robert was the one they were looking for. Stella probably knew a lot of Texas men who drove black trucks. More than likely, he's the one Turner is looking for. But why should she help the sheriff after he assured her that he could do the job? And why should she make more trouble for the man who was nearly in tears last night talking about Stella? Emily felt sorry for him. She sipped the hot coffee. Fluffy came bouncing out to the kitchen. Emily picked her up and put her outside, grateful the cat hadn't had an overnight accident yet in the cabin.

The air was still cool and damp, and Emily decided to walk down to the resort's office to get a newspaper. Since she didn't have to be at the marina until two P.M., she could have a lazy morning again. "This hasn't been the worst assignment in the world," she said to herself. Emily decided to give the idea of calling the sheriff a little more thought. She put on her running suit and went out for a walk. As she walked past her rental car, she gave it a once-over glance, the way Jim always reminded her to do: "Every time you see your car, look at the tires to make sure you're not getting a flat." The tires looked fine, but scrawled in the damp dust of the rear window were the words "Get out of town, bitch." Emily stared at the message. Who would have written that? Robert? It must be Robert. But why would he have written that? He wasn't angry with me last night. We're supposed to go out tonight. Who else knows where I'm staying? She answered herself right away: probably everyone in town. She'd told Lyle and Monica and John Hackett. And the sheriff knew. But she hadn't heard any cars drive up last night. She hadn't heard Robert's car leave, either. Now she had to tell the sheriff. She headed back into the cabin, trying to think of what to say.

"Someone wrote something dirty on my car," she imagined telling the sheriff. "I think it might have been the guy you're looking for. He's been staying next door to me. I've been dancing with him, he's kissed me, we got drunk together last night, and we have a date for tonight." Oh, that would sound great. Maybe she'd call anonymously. But then what would she say? "I think I saw the guy you're looking for, but I don't think he did it, and I never saw the license number of his truck and I don't know where he is today." Swell.

The best thing was just to tell the truth, even if he didn't listen to her, she decided and dialed the sheriff's department number. It was busy. That must be an omen, Emily thought. I'll try it later. Maybe.

Emily took a quick shower, tossed her one-piece swimsuit, a towel, and her sunscreen in her purse, and donned

126

the only pair of shorts she'd brought. Then she tried the sheriff's number again. I'll just tell him about the threat on my car, she thought. As the phone was ringing, she had second thoughts and hung up. He's going to make me feel like a fool. Then, So what. Someone's harassing me, threatening me, and he should know about it. She dialed again.

"This is Emily Stone," she said. "I need to speak to Sheriff Turner. I'll hold."

"What can I do for you?" he asked brusquely when he came on the line.

"Sheriff," Emily started, already feeling foolish, "I wanted to report that someone wrote a threatening message in the dust on the back window of my car last night. It says, Get out of town, bitch." She could almost feel the sheriff repressing a smile.

"Where was your car parked, ma'am?" he asked.

"It was outside my cabin here at the Bitterroot. It's made me really nervous, and I just wanted to tell you in case anything else should happen."

"Did you see or hear anything unusual last night, or do you have any idea who may have done this?"

Emily hesitated. Really, the answer to both those questions was no, and she just couldn't bring herself to get into the whole story of Robert. "No," she said.

There was silence on the line for a moment.

"Well, thank you for reporting this, ma'am," the sheriff said. "I wouldn't be too worried about it. Most rental cars have the company's name on the car. You'll probably notice that on yours, and as you might expect, not everyone in town is happy about the tourists who come here. It might have been just a kid who did it on a dare or something like that. There's a car wash about three blocks east of the sheriff's department. And if anything else happens feel free to call me."

"Thank you," Emily said, and hung up. The conversation had gone better than she'd expected, but it hadn't accomplished a thing. At least the sheriff had been polite. Maybe it *had* been kids. She remembered an afternoon when she'd returned to the cabin and passed a carload of boys, probably high school age, driving out of the resort. Maybe they cruised the lake looking for chicks in swimsuits. She went outside and looked at her car again. Sure enough, there on the back bumper was a sticker that said "This car courtesy of Budget Rentals." The sheriff could be right.

One thing she could do for herself was to change to another hotel. And not tell anyone this time. She started calling the nicer-sounding places advertised in the phone book, but there were no vacancies. A lot of places were sold out because of Friday's awards show, one desk clerk told her. In all, she called more than twenty motels, cabins, and lodges. None had a room. Well, so far nothing serious had happened. It was probably just some teenagers thinking they'd be funny. And besides, she'd seen Robert packing, and he'd said his truck repairs were supposed to be finished today, so maybe he wouldn't even be back. She had no intention of being at Rocky's tonight, and she was willing to bet he'd never remember the date he'd made, either.

Grow up, Emily said to herself. You're a big girl. You've got a gun. Stop being paranoid.

On the other hand, maybe paranoia was healthy in this situation. She chided herself for her indecisiveness and sat down at the table. The best way to figure out what to do was to write things down, she had found. Putting it on paper often cleared away confusion. At home, tucked away in her nightstand drawer, was a list of pros and cons about Jim. The evening she had made that list, the reasons for staying with him had been much longer than the reasons to end their relationship. Now, at the top of a sheet of

128

paper, Emily wrote: "Suspects in Stella's Death." The first name she wrote was Robert Simmons. She gave him one plus mark beside his name. John and Irene Hackett each got a plus mark, and so did Monica. Despite her apparent sorrow at Stella's death, there was something she wanted to hide. Then she wrote: "Others?" Good thing Emily had never set out to become a detective. But Monica was the only one on the list she hadn't discussed with Turner, so she called him back.

"It's Emily Stone again. I thought of another thing you should know. On Monday while I was driving around town, I saw Monica Deal go into Stella Love's trailer. I knew it was Stella's place because her name was on the mailbox. When she came out, she was carrying a bundle of papers. Stella must have been a threat to Monica's career, and I'm pretty sure she was upstairs at the Hacketts' when the accident happened. I just thought you should know."

"Did you ask Monica why she'd gone to Stella's? Maybe she'd loaned Stella things that she needed to get back."

"No, I didn't talk to Monica," Emily said, omitting that she'd been lurking in the bushes.

"I'll look into it," Turner said evenly. "Thank you for your help."

"You're welcome," Emily said, but Turner had already hung up. At least she'd done her civic duty.

Emily found the car wash three blocks east of the sheriff's department. It was the kind where you put your money in a slot and drive the car through yourself. She was relieved there were no attendants to snicker over the message on the back. When the car was shiny again, Emily drove down by the lake and stopped at a small cafe she'd seen on Monday. The sign outside Windy City Dogs advertised Chicago–Style Hot Dogs with All the Trimmings. In contrast to the business-lunch crowd at McGuffey's, here everyone wore shorts and carried cameras. A chubby woman took a picture of her chubby husband taking a bite of a huge, greasy hamburger. Emily hoped no photo would record her biting into the hot dog topped with pickle relish, chopped onions, tangy sport peppers, sliced tomatoes, and a dill pickle spear.

As Emily ate, she looked out the window at the lake and watched a paddle-wheeler excursion boat glide by. If I worked in Branson, I'd come here for lunch every day, Emily thought idly. The hot dog was so good that Emily went back and ordered another. She was nearly finished when it dawned on her that she was headed for a boat ride, but it was too late now to worry about getting seasick.

She got to the marina just before two P.M. Hackett wasn't kidding when he told her to look for the biggest houseboat at the docks. The *Good Times* towered over the other boats. Sleek and white, the boat's flying bridge nearly touched the roof of the boat slip. Emily could see people on the front deck of the boat. She supposed they'd all be thrilled to see the reporter come aboard. Then she saw Lyle's familiar figure come on deck from the cabin. At least she'd have one friend on board.

Lyle did seem happy to see her and gave her a big hug after helping her step aboard the ship. Emily was surprised that he wasn't wearing his traditional denim overalls, but a red T-shirt and plaid Bermuda shorts. His legs were pale and nearly hairless, skinny. He looked as if he'd been mounted on toothpicks. "You look comfortable today." Emily grinned.

"Well, I'm not," Lyle said, hitching up the shorts that hung under his belly. "I get so used to wearing my costume that I nearly forget who I am if I dress like a normal person. But then who ever said I was a normal person?" Lyle chuckled.

Just then, Irene came out of the cabin to greet her.

130

Emily was surprised that Irene seemed genuinely pleased to see her. She looked more vital today, even a little tan.

Irene offered her a tour of the boat. As she led Emily toward the front cabin, she shooed away a big yellow cat that had just jumped onto the houseboat's deck from the dock. "That's Polly, the marina's mouse catcher," Irene said, smiling. "If you don't watch her, you end up with her on board all day in the middle of the lake."

The boat was a beauty. Twelve people could sleep on board. The front cabin was as well decorated as any stylish living room. An L-shaped couch covered with maroon upholstery wrapped around a coffee table set with bowls of sugar-coated nuts and a tray of vegetables with dip. Pink shrimp were piled on a silver tray. A lighted cabinet with etched-glass doors filled one wall and displayed silver goblets and animals carved from crystal. The cabinet also held stereo gear, a large television, and a VCR. The floors were carpeted, save a tiled walkway the length of the boat. The compact kitchen area contained glass-fronted cabinets, a range and microwave, and a good-size refrigerator. Irene showed Emily side-by-side built-ins, one an icemaker, one a trash compactor.

There were two bathrooms on the main deck, one with a full-size tiled shower. The Captain's Quarters held a queen-size bunk, a mirrored dressing table, and had more closet space than her apartment, Emily noticed. Below the main deck were two more bedrooms, smaller but still luxuriously appointed, and another bathroom. Emily had seen big houseboats moored at marinas along Tampa's Sun Coast, but she had never been aboard one.

"Irene, this is just beautiful," Emily said. "I'd be tempted just to live out here."

"I do sneak off and stay out here sometimes," Irene confessed. "It's so peaceful, especially at night." Irene leaned close to Emily and cupped her hand to her mouth as though about to tell a secret. "I like to come out here and write," she said quietly. Emily didn't understand why Irene would say it like that. She was going to ask when Irene continued in a normal tone. "But it can be awfully damp living on the water, too. Everything's damp in the mornings."

Irene seemed much more relaxed than she was last weekend. Emily wondered if she was relieved that Stella would not be at this party.

Irene got Emily a cold beer and told her to make herself at home, adding that they'd be under way as soon as John arrived. "I don't know why he's late," Irene said, looking at her watch. When she excused herself to greet arriving guests, Emily went into the largest bathroom and changed into her swimsuit. She carried her beer up to the top deck, where a couple of women in swimsuits lay in chaise lounges on the part of the deck not shaded by the boat slip's roof.

The lake was smooth as Mylar without a breeze to ruffle the surface. Emily leaned back in her chair and closed her eyes. From nearby speakers, the sound of soft jazz floated out over the water. Emily wished Jim were with her. He'd really enjoy this place, she thought. I should call him tonight. I could call him right now. I'm sure this boat even has a fax machine hidden in some cabinet.

It was nearly three o'clock by the time John Hackett made his noisy arrival, spreading apologies for his tardiness. Hackett wore a bright Hawaiian print shirt, white shorts, and—of course—a captain's cap. Emily stayed on the top deck and watched Hackett make his way around the main deck, untying the ropes that held them in the slip. When he reached the rear of the boat, he saw Polly the dock cat stretched out in the sun. John didn't kick the cat. He just lifted it with the toe of his deck shoe and heaved it over the side of the boat into the lake. Emily was horrified to see the cat hit the water. She almost called out, but stopped herself in time when she saw that a young man on the dock also had seen the cat in the lake. Emily watched the cat's head bob up and down in the water while it fought to stay afloat. She saw the boy on the dock climb down a ladder to the water, calling and holding his hand out to the cat, who was floundering in his direction. Then Emily heard the boat's engine start. The boat slid out of the slip and turned toward the open water. Emily could see as they pulled away that the cat was slowly closing the distance to the boy on the ladder.

Her instinct was to confront Hackett, to chew him out for tossing the cat in the water. But that would be futile, she thought. And maybe really stupid. I'll just keep my distance from him. It was probably a mistake to come on this trip today anyway. The breeze generated by the boat's movement was refreshing and Emily pushed her hair back from her face, tucking it behind her ears. But here I am. I might as well try to enjoy it.

Emily judged there were about thirty people on the boat. Some she recognized from the Jacketts' party and some were new faces. Among them were several cute young women, all in bikinis. Now a Latin American rhythm filtered through the speakers around the boat, mingled with the sounds of laughter. After ten minutes, the boat reached the center of the lake and Hackett turned off the engines. Emily had expected more boat traffic on a warm summer day, but it was such a big lake, nine hundred miles of shoreline. It was wide in some places and long and narrow in the areas where it followed the course of the dammed-up White River that lay buried under tons of water. Fishermen were probably off in the many coves that jutted off from the main body of water, and those visitors who rented boats or the noisy jet skis from the marina stayed closer to shore.

On the top deck, Emily had been joined by three of the bikini beauties, who were lying facedown on loungers, mindful only of the sun cooking their oiled skin. Emily wandered downstairs. She saw Irene and Monica sitting on the rear deck, their heads close together in conversation. Both women wore shorts and tank tops. Emily took a nearby chair just behind the two, intending to join the conversation, but they were too engrossed to notice her. Instead of greeting them, she found herself listening.

"She was just buried yesterday, Irene," Monica said. "And I couldn't even go to the funeral. I just had to stand by while they shipped her back to Texas. I wonder if anyone was there? From the minute she showed up at my door last April, I knew she was her mother's daughter. All my drive, no talent, and not a brain in her head." Monica rubbed suntan lotion on her arms.

"There was nothing you could have done," Irene reassured her. "We all make mistakes when we're young. Even if you'd stayed home and raised her, you couldn't have protected her every minute. Accidents just happen and you've got to stop dwelling on it like this, Monica."

Now Emily understood Monica's red eyes the day after Stella Love's death. Stella hadn't just been casual competition for Monica's job.

"When I think back on the day I signed the adoption papers—" Monica said, her voice choking. "It all came back to me so clearly when I took them from her trailer."

"Don't think back," Irene said, putting her hand on Monica's arm. "You can't change the past. All you can do is go on. You knew from the day she came back that she wasn't here for a sentimental reunion with her mother. She was here because she found out her mother was a star and she thought she could force you to help her because of guilt. Monica, she was like a stranger to you. And not a very nice person, either. You had nothing to do with that.

She might have ruined you if she'd stayed here. I know that's a harsh way to look at it, but it's true." Irene's voice grew low and Emily was surprised at the hard edge in it. "Things work out for the best sometimes when you least expect it, Monica."

Just then, a woman's high-pitched giggle broke the mood. The three women turned to see Hackett, his arm around the waist of a bikini-clad redhead, go down the steps into the lower cabins. Monica and Irene also saw Emily sitting behind them.

"Excuse me," Irene said without a smile. She got up and walked back toward the main cabin. Without a word, Monica turned her back to Emily and sat staring out over the lake. Emily couldn't think of a thing to say, so she just stared at the lake, too. She wanted to say something to Monica. Emily thought about the period in her youth when she believed she was an adopted child. "Not an uncommon fantasy for a child," her psychologist had reassured her. Emily hadn't mentioned to him that it happened when she was beyond childhood, after her father's death and into her early teens. She had been convinced that she could not possibly be related to her mother, and she would lie in bed at night wishing her real mother would come get her and that they'd go and find her father and be one big, happy family. Emily got up and went to help herself to another beer from the refrigerator in the galley.

In the largest of the cabins below deck, John Hackett was sitting on the bunk, kissing the woman in the pink bikini. His right hand held a mass of her curly coppery hair. His left hand roved across her back, brushed her narrow waist, and settled on the mound of her breast.

"You're so sweet, baby." John was breathing heavily; sweat trickled down the side of his face. "Be my candy, baby." Then he pulled away from the woman, stood up, and motioned for her to lie back on the bed. He arranged her hair, fanning it out over the pillow. As though he were directing a movie, he told her to turn her face a little toward him. Hackett leaned against the wall at the foot of the bunk and gave instructions. "Spread your legs out, sweetheart," he said. "Point those pretty little toes. Put your hands up there and show me just a little nipple. That's right, baby, just pull it down and tease me. That's right. That's good. Now run your hands down lower. Feel that tight tummy? Feel how warm the sun made it? Now slip your fingers into that bikini. In a little farther. That's good. Doesn't that feel good? Let me see how good it feels. Do it for me, baby. Give your old man a pretty show."

Emily walked from the galley out to the deck's railing. She looked toward the windows in the downstairs cabin. All the blinds were drawn. Just then, Lyle Malone stepped onto the deck and came over to her.

"Well, are you enjoying our little lake?" he asked.

"As usual, I'm learning a lot of new things," Emily said. "Who's the redhead John has downstairs?"

Lyle glanced toward the lower deck. He didn't answer Emily, but took his flask of Southern Comfort from the pocket of his baggy shorts and took a swig. Then he walked to the stairway and called, "Hey, where's the captain of this ship? You're wanted on deck, Captain."

When there was no response, Lyle pounded on the wall of the stairwell. "Captain John's wanted on deck," he called louder. A moment later, Emily heard Hackett's voice.

"Goddammit, Lyle," Hackett said. "What the hell do you want?"

Lyle took a couple of steps down the stairway. Emily could barely hear him.

"I want you to turn off your camera and let that

woman out of there," Lyle said. "Or maybe you'd rather I just brought Irene down here?"

"All right, all right," Hackett said. "I'll be up in a minute. Don't do anything you'll regret, Lyle. You know what I'm talking about."

Lyle came back upstairs and leaned against the railing next to Emily.

"What was that all about?" Emily asked.

"You don't want to know," Lyle said. "You've stayed too long and you're getting to know us too well. I guess we're like people in every other small town. We all have some secrets in closets."

As Lyle was mopping his brow, Emily heard a beep from one of Lyle's pockets. He unfolded the compact phone and held it to his ear. "Okay. Let me find out and I'll call you right back," he said.

"Business," Lyle said to Emily. "I ought to throw this in the lake." Lyle turned and walked back toward the crowd in the main cabin. A moment later, the redhead minced up the steps from below and continued on to the top deck. Then Hackett came up into the sunshine and spotted Emily.

Why did Emily think of a quivering pile of snakes every time she looked at him?

"Having a good time?" he asked. "Finding enough to eat? How about champagne?"

"I'm fine, really," Emily said.

"Have you seen the rest of the boat?" he asked. He put a hand, cool and soft, on her forearm. Emily reacted instantly, pulling her arm close to her, but the hand stayed on her. Now it was nearly touching her breast. Emily didn't move a muscle. She looked Hackett straight in the eye, or tried to. The gaping pupil made it difficult to know which eye to focus on. Hackett didn't move, either. A trickle of

sweat ran down his forehead and dangled from his eye-
brow.

"Your wife already showed me the boat," Emily said
icily.

"Well, good. She's the perfect little hostess, isn't she?
But she's delicate. I'm sure you wouldn't say anything to
upset her, would you? I can be very protective." He tightened his grip on her arm until it hurt, then released it. "I
guess I'll go try that champagne. You'd better get some,
Ms. Reporter." He walked away from her.

This is definitely my last John Hackett party, Emily
thought, letting out the breath she'd been holding. I can't
wait to get away from these crazy people. Let them solve
their own sordid problems. I hope my next assignment is
to a peaceful deserted island.

Emily was ready to leave the boat long before Hackett
started the engines and headed back for the dock. The sun
was low and already the air temperature had cooled. The
bikinied women had donned fashionable cover-ups, and
Irene sat by herself on the rear deck, the collar of her
windbreaker hiding most of her face. Emily didn't know
where Monica had gone. She hadn't seen her for an hour.

When the boat pulled into the slip, Emily was one of
the first to disembark. She didn't seek out Lyle or even
Irene to thank her. She just wanted to be away from the
entire seedy bunch. Whatever problems they had, she
didn't want to know about them. Two more days and she'd
be out of here.

Emily was tired and the drive back to the cabin seemed to take forever. As usual, there was no one around. And no pickup or car parked next door. Emily pulled in, leaned back in the car, and rubbed her temples. Too much sun, too many beers. She wanted a cool shower. Her head was spinning with unanswered questions that she didn't even want to ask. She'd see if there was a good flick on pay-per-view tonight, she thought as she turned the lock on her cabin.

She had stepped inside and closed the door before she noticed the scent. The maid must have gone a little wild with the disinfectant, she thought. She slipped off her shoes and pulled off her shorts, which she hung on a peg in the closet. Glancing around to make sure all the curtains were drawn, she walked over to the hole she had filled with Kleenex. The tissue was gone. Fluffy must have played with that last night, or Super Maid got it, Emily thought as she replugged the opening with a new tissue. Emily took off her watch and bracelet and carried them to the kitchen table where she put them in a saucer that held some change and a paper clip. Then she stopped dead in her tracks. The scrap of shiny fabric that she'd found in the driveway no longer lay in the saucer. Emily looked on the floor under the table. She thought again of the kitten. But a chill crept up her back, along her neck and into the roots of her hair. The quiet of the cabin pressed against her. The notes stacked on the table lay in five neat piles, their edges perfectly aligned. The brochures also rested in a tidy stack and her list of suspects was where she had left it. Her reporter's notebook was closed. But the piles of papers looked neater, perfectly straight. They had been stacked more loosely. She moved to the nightstand and slowly pulled open the top drawer. The gun rested on a towel, right where it had been. Or was it turned a little? She checked the loaded gun.

"Stop," she told herself. "These hillbillies are driving you crazy."

Emily checked the lock on the front door again. Nothing that she could see showed signs of a forced entry. It must have been the maid, she tried to convince herself. Taking a cool shower, Emily could feel where the sun had pinkened her arms and the tops of her legs, and she closed her eyes and pictured the water putting out the fire.

While Emily flicked through the television channels, she thought of calling Jim. She picked up the phone twice, but hung it up without dialing. She paged through her Robert Browning book, but couldn't land on anything she wanted to read again. She watched part of *Key Largo* and some old war movie. Finally, while the *Home Shopping* host was displaying a lovely garnet ring, Emily fell asleep.

In Emily's dream, Jim and John Hackett were swimming in a lake of English Leather. The water was dark brown and the men were treading water and shouting at each other. Emily couldn't understand them. "Tell me what's wrong," she shouted at them from the shore. Then a driving rain hit, churning the waters and blinding Emily. "Where are you?" she called again and again. She saw a figure floating toward her in the turbid water, just out of reach. Emily waded out toward the object, holding out her arms to ward off the rain. As she reached her hands toward it, the figure bobbed to the surface. In her dream, Emily screamed as she saw the bloated yellow cat, its sightless eyes white and staring at her.

The nightmare woke Emily. She jumped out of bed and turned on all the lights and turned off the static on the television. A crack of thunder made her jump, and she peeked through the curtains. Outside, lightning flashed and the rain came down in sheets. Emily opened the door a crack and softly called, "Kitty, kitty?" There was no answer and she closed the door, crawled between the sheets, and put the pillow over her head.

Across town, a flash of lightning illuminated Irene Hackett's face. Above the dying rumble of thunder, Irene heard a soft knock on her bedroom door.

"Come in," Irene called. She laid the book she had been reading next to her on the bed. The light from the nightstand lamp shimmered in the crystal statue of the rabbit below. Irene leaned back against the pale blue pillows and pulled up the strap of her cotton nightgown. John came through the door.

"I just wanted to tell you that I propped something against that shutter downstairs, so it won't be banging in the wind anymore. Everything all right up here?"

"Yes," Irene said. She waited to see what he was going to say next. He saw her waiting.

"I should have had someone fix that hinge last week," he said. "I thought I had it tightened up." He walked over to the window and pulled on the drapery cord to shut the curtains.

"It feels like fall tonight," he said. "Listen to it rain. I put the cars in the garage. When was it we had that hailstorm last spring?"

"April, I think," she said.

"We were lucky it didn't get the greenhouse." He walked over and sat down on the edge of the bed on her side, halfway up. He patted her hand. "I haven't seen much of you for a few days," he said. "You've been in and out a lot."

"Well, I was with you on the houseboat all day. You were the one who was *out.*" John stood up and walked to the foot of the bed. "What do you mean by that?"

"I just meant I didn't see much of you today." Irene plucked at the blanket. She looked around the room. For a minute she stared at the painting of two women feeding a flock of ducks. John waited. "I mean, Stella was one thing. People knew she was working for you, that you were trying to help her career. I let her in the house and went out of my way to try to make friends with her." Her hands worked at the fuzz. "I didn't even know those girls on the boat. I don't think they knew who I was, either." Irene stopped and looked up at him.

"I'm sorry," he said. He stood with his hands in his pockets. "What do you want me to say? I'm sorry. I just got a little carried away. This hasn't exactly been easy for me either, you know." He paced to the far side of the room.

"I don't mind so much that you keep the cabin out there," she said. "No one really knows about that. You've been *discreet*. Don't you think that's an especially good idea right now?"

"What do you mean?" The pitch of John's voice was higher than his normal rasp.

"I just mean that you have to be careful. You can't just go around with *anybody.*"

"Yeah, and it's pretty hard to go around with *anyone* if you can't *get it up,* right?" His voice was whining, rising. "Isn't that what you meant?" Hackett came back to stand at the end of the bed. His face was red.

"No," Irene said. "That wasn't what I was talking about. You only have a problem if you think you do. You make things worse for yourself by worrying about it so much."

"I'm sorry," he said, more softly. "I seem to be sorry a lot lately."

"I just wish you'd be careful. That's all," she said quietly. "You hardly spoke to me on the boat. Everybody saw you going downstairs with that . . . that girl."

"I was just showing her around," John said, pacing across the room. "It didn't mean I was doing anything."

"But it's the way it looked. Don't you think people are already talking about us enough?"

"I have friends," he said loudly. "You know I have a lot of friends and some of them just happen to be young women. I can't help it if you want to just hole up in the house and write your damned poetry."

Irene glared at him. "I have a lot more fun spending my time with Robert Frost than I do with you."

"I guess you had fun spending a little time with our friendly sheriff on Sunday, didn't you?" Hackett watched Irene as he paced.

Her expression didn't change. "You have someone following me these days? I had a quick lunch with Ron. Apparently you know that. What difference does it make?"

"What did you talk about? Old times? Did you tell him the old man's gone bad on you, and you wished you'd married Ron to begin with?"

"He wanted to warn me about that reporter. She's been asking questions about Stella and us. Who knows what she'll write. You were a fool to invite her on the boat. Don't talk to her anymore."

"Maybe you should have married him," John said. "I'm sure he'd still take you. He's always wanted you. Why don't you go back to him? Let him take care of you and buy you jewelry and a beautiful house and nice cars. I'm sure he could do that real well on his sheriff's salary."

Irene's eyes narrowed. "Didn't you hear me? She's dangerous. She thinks Stella was blackmailing you by threatening to tell people you were impotent."

John stopped packing. "How do you know that? Did she tell you that? How could she have known that?"

"She told Ron that she'd heard a rumor. You tell me. How could she have heard that rumor?"

John rubbed his chin, ran his fingers through his greasy hair. "Maybe she overheard us at the cabin."

"What do you mean?"

"The last time I met Stella out at the resort, we had a fight. Stella was screaming at me. How was I supposed to know there was a reporter staying out there? What are we going to do? I have to stop her."

"You're a fool, John. Stay away from her. Do you hear me?"

"So Ron knows I can't be a husband to you anymore? He'll really be after you now. I'm going to tell him he'd better keep his distance. I'll be watching him. I'll have my friends watching him. Don't forget what I've given you."

"I could divorce you right now and keep the jewelry and the house and the cars," Irene said evenly. "I have friends in town, too, you know."

"Divorce?" John shouted. He stopped pacing. "What are you talking about? I never heard you say that word before, Irene." John walked back to the window and took hold of the edge of the curtain. He tried to pull it open by its edge, but it didn't budge.

"How can you even say that? What are you trying to punish me for?" He tugged harder at the curtain. "You wouldn't last two weeks without me. I take care of everything for you." He jerked at the curtain and Irene heard the sound of fabric tearing.

144

John walked to the closet door and kicked it. "You wouldn't know what to do. You'd be crawling back in a week. Why are you talking like this?" He came toward her.

Irene slid down a little in the bed. John grabbed her shoulder and shook her. "Why are you saying these things?"

Irene pushed his arm away and flipped back the covers and stood up. She shoved him backward with both her hands against his chest. He came back at her and grabbed her wrists, pulling her toward him.

"Stop it," he said, shaking her by the wrists. "Stop it. Stop it." His face was red and distorted. Then he was crying, sobbing. He put his face against her fists, still holding her arms. "Don't," he sobbed. "Don't."

Irene pulled her wrists out of his grasp and took his face in her hands. She pressed it to her chest and put her arms around him. He put his arms around her and stood there, his head lowered against her, crying like a baby.

"Stop," Irene said softly. "Stop. It's all right." She patted his back, rocking him gently.

"Here." She pushed him toward the bed and pulled tissues from the box on the nightstand. "Blow your nose," she said. He sat down. His eyes were red.

Irene sat down beside him and took him in her arms again. He turned and held her. They both flinched as the clap of thunder echoed through the room.

"Sleep in here tonight," she said to him. "Take your clothes off and crawl in here next to me."

Silently, he did as he was told, dropping his clothes in a pile beside the bed. They got under the blankets and she held him in her arms, his head against her shoulder.

In a minute, he had stopped trembling. "You won't leave me, will you?" he asked, his voice more husky than normal.

"I won't leave you, John," she said. She stroked his

head. "I just want you to be careful. I just worry about you."

John kissed her neck and snuggled closer to her. With one arm still around his shoulders, Irene reached down and got the book and dropped it onto the floor beside the bed. She turned off the lamp and slid down in bed, holding him to her, rocking him.

"Just stay close," she murmured.

Outside, the storm rumbled off toward the northeast. It passed over the Hacketts' mansion, dumping no hail on the greenhouse. The storm sent sheets of water into the lake, bobbling the boats in the marina as if they were toys in a tub. In the last flash of lightning over the north side of town, Monica looked at the man who lay beside her in bed. His back was turned away from her.

"Are you sleeping?" she asked softly.

She saw the muscles in his back ripple as he turned over on his side to face her. He stroked her cheek with his finger.

"I like your hair better like this," he said, and pushed his fingers through Monica's baby-fine pale brown hair. "I don't know why you bother with wigs, baby."

Monica pulled herself up, holding the sheet against her breasts. She leaned back against the pillow and pushed back a stray strand of hair.

"Because it's too thin," she said. "It's mousy-looking, and I can't get it to do anything but just lie there. I'll probably end up bald, like some of those old women you see on the strip."

"You'll still be beautiful," Robert said.

"Would you stop it?" Monica said. "I don't know what to think about this anyway without you adding sweet talk to it."

"Didn't you like it?" Robert asked.

Monica put her hand on his bare shoulder. "Yes, I

liked it." She smiled. "It was the best thing that's happened to me in a very long time. But you're my daughter's lover. And you're way too young for me. I'm old enough to be your mother. Nearly old enough." Monica pulled the sheet up a little higher. "When I see something like this happen on a soap opera, I just think it's sick, you know? I certainly never thought about you like this."

"Never?" Robert smiled. Monica smiled back at him.

"Well, I might have thought about it once," she said. "You know what a good-looking devil you are. But I never thought I'd do anything about it."

"Until tonight, right? About an hour ago?" Robert said, still grinning.

"I'm going downstairs to get something to drink," Monica said. She turned her back to him and reached for a robe that lay in a heap on the floor. She put it on and stood up, gathering the robe in front of her, reaching for the ties in the dimness from the hall light. "Do you want anything?"

"Just for you to hurry back, sugar," he said.

"I don't know if I can handle this," she said. She turned and went out of the room.

In the kitchen, Monica got a glass and turned on the tap. She stood with her finger under the running water, waiting for the rust she imagined filled the old pipes to clear. Then she filled the glass and took a swallow. She turned around and saw Robert standing in the kitchen doorway, his arms folded across his chest. His naked body in the soft light from the street lamp outside made her think of the men she'd seen on calendars. His shoulders were wide, his hips narrow, his legs muscular. He was tan except where a brief swimsuit had left him pale. It had been a long time since she'd seen such a beautiful male body standing naked in her kitchen, and Monica admired the view.

"Want a drink of water?" she asked.

"I don't need any water," he said. "Come back to bed."

He crossed the room. When he got close, she turned her back and poured the rest of the water into the sink. Robert came up behind her and put his arms around her. He held her tightly. His arms felt good, and Monica closed her eyes, trying not to think about whose arms they were. It didn't work for long.

"What would Stella think?" she whispered to him.

"Stella wouldn't care," he whispered back. He turned her to face him and kissed her gently on the lips.

"Stella's gone," he said quietly. "We're both sorry, but there was nothing we could have done to stop it. And there's nothing we can do to change this now, either. This just happened. Life is what happens while you're making other plans, you know? I didn't plan this."

"Are you sure?" Monica said, looking up at him.

He gave her a squeeze, then let go. He picked up the glass in the sink, ran the water and took a drink.

"I came by here tonight because you said I could stay here if I needed to. I thought my car was going to be finished today and now I can't get it until tomorrow. And then like a fool I got drunk last night and told that reporter I'd been a friend of Stella's, and who knows if she passed that on to the sheriff. All I know is I don't want to get picked up and put through a bunch of crap if I can avoid it. So I thought I'd come here. The rest of it just happened."

"It was stupid to say anything to that reporter," Monica said. "What else did you tell her?"

"Well, nothing really," Robert said. "I just got off talking about how women never listen to a man's advice."

"Did you say anything about me?" Monica asked.

"No, honey, I didn't." Robert reached out to put his arm around Monica, but she pulled back and moved a little away from him.

"Did you tell her I was Stella's mother?"

"No," Robert said. "I didn't say anything about you, I told you. You think I'm lying to you?"

"No," Monica said. "I just don't want anyone else in this town knowing about it. It's not something I'm proud of, and my fans wouldn't take too well to a *National Enquirer* story about how I'd given my daughter away and drove her to her death. I can see those headlines." Monica stared at Robert. "Someone could make a lot of money selling that story," she said quietly.

"You're not looking at me, are you?" Robert watched her. "You are. You think I'd do a thing like that." Robert ran his hand over his chest. "Honey, how could you even think that? You know I wouldn't do anything to hurt you," he said. His deep voice grew louder. "If you think I'm just some money-grubbing bum who's looking for a handout, I'll just take my raggedy ass out of here right now. I believed what you said about helping me stay in Branson." His voice went quiet again. "That's all I was thinking about until I got over here tonight and saw you looking so beautiful. You could seduce a dead man, darlin."

"I wasn't trying to seduce you. I never even thought that you'd be interested in an old lady like me."

"There you go again, fishing for a compliment," he teased.

"I'm not," she said.

"So how old are you, anyway?" he asked. "Why don't we just get this age thing figured out and get past it?"

Monica went over to the refrigerator and opened the door. She reached in for a wedge of cheese. "I don't want to tell you," she said. "You've never heard such a high number."

"All right, then I'll have to guess," Robert said. He sat down at the kitchen table. "Fifty-five."

"I'm not!" Monica said, reaching in the cupboard for

crackers. She took a knife out of a drawer and went to the table. "I'll never be that old."

"Fifty."

"You're a shit," she said, slicing off two pieces of cheese. She put one on a cracker and handed it to him. "How old are you?"

"I'm almost twenty-nine," Robert said.

"I had to give up saying that a few years ago. If I tell you I'm . . . in my forties, for example, you'll tell me that age doesn't really make any difference, that you're only as old as you feel, that between two people it's just the feelings that count," Monica said. "I started hearing that from men a while back. When I was younger, I used to hear the line about how small breasts are nice. 'Anything more than a mouthful's a waste.' I got tired of hearing it." Monica took a bite of cheese and cracker.

Robert swallowed. He was looking at the red silk robe stretched over her ample, firm bosom.

"Forty-one," he said. "Forty-two." He was grinning at her. "Forty-three."

"I'm forty-six," Monica snapped. "Happy now?"

Robert did imaginary math in the air with his finger. "To be my mother, you would have had to have me when you were eighteen," he said. "That's too young for a smart lady like you to have been having babies. So, see, you're not old enough to be my mother. Feel better?"

"I was twenty-three when I had Stella," Monica said quietly. "I wasn't a smart lady."

Robert took her hand. "You told me you didn't want to give her up," he said. "I believe you. You did what you thought you had to do at the time. That's all you can ask of a person. Monica, you can't keep beating yourself up about the past. We have to go on."

Monica pulled his hand to her lips and kissed it. "I know we do, Robert. And I will. It's just going to take me a little while to get this straightened out in my mind."

"And I'll be here to help you, baby," he said, "if you'll just let me stay for a while. Maybe you could ask about a job at the theater, just until I get things straightened out, too. All right?"

Monica stood up and wrapped up the cheese and put it back in the refrigerator. She looked at Robert, sitting at the table watching her.

"All right," she said. "Just for a while."

★ *13* ★

When Emily woke up, her nightstand clock said it was nearly noon. She could barely believe she'd slept so late. Then she remembered the storm and that she'd had a bad dream, but she couldn't recall what it had been about. It had taken her a long time to go back to sleep. But it didn't matter that she'd slept late. I've got the whole day to kill, she thought, and then grimaced at her choice of words. Let's see if I can get through an entire day here without thinking about killing or death. I don't know anything. I don't know if Stella fell or was pushed. I don't know that anyone did anything to her. And no one's done anything to me, so just relax.

There was no sign of last night's storm. The sky was blue as always and Emily decided to drive to the little village of Rocky Shores, about forty miles east of Branson. She'd read about the town, how it had been the first real tourist town in the area years ago when people came for fishing along Lake Taneycomo. Back in the 1920s, the town drew a wealthy class of tourists from the cities. It was said there were speakeasies where local moonshine fueled some wild parties. After Prohibition, the town faded into a quaint resort, a quiet place for families until the late 1960s, when the Hell's Angels decided to hold their annual meeting there. One account said there had been so much trouble in town one summer that the resort never recovered its tourist trade.

On the way to Rocky Shores, Emily passed through rolling hills that here and there gave way to rocky bluffs. She pulled over into a Scenic View turnoff and looked across the valley a mile below, where Lake Taneycomo snaked along the same path the river had once followed. In fact, Emily thought, it looked more like a river than a lake.

Coming down the curvy two-lane road into the town, Emily felt as if she'd driven into a time warp. No new motels here, no bulldozing going on. The main drag, spanning about a mile of lakefront, was lined with a dozen or so resorts clustered side by side. The only way to tell where one resort ended and the next began was by the colors of the cabins. Here was a cluster painted deep forest-green. Next door, half a dozen fire-engine-red cabins dolled up with white shutters. Fortunately, the several cabins bearing robin's-egg-blue paint were separated from the red and green groups by a section of cabins painted white. Most of them bore the gingerbread trim fashionable in the 1950s. It was like coming into a valley of Easter eggs. She turned and cruised slowly by the nest of cabins again, wondering if they had waited for paint to be on sale, or if there had been a town contest one year.

The resort names reflected the reasons people must have come to stay here: The Hideaway, Fishermens Camp, Wildcat Roost. Cars were parked beside some of the cabins, but she saw only a few people around, most of them fishing from the banks along the lakefront. There wasn't much activity anywhere in town. Emily pulled into a parking space in front of the Lake Restaurant cafe.

"Original thinkers, these folks," Emily said to herself. The restaurant looked clean inside and the welcome smell of coffee greeted Emily. Big windows lined the back wall, giving a long view of the narrow lake. Across from the restaurant, rocky cliffs rose a hundred feet. Here and there, nestled on a rocky ledge, Emily saw bright clumps of what looked like purple daisies swaying in the breeze. She knew they were coneflowers, and wondered how she'd known that. Then she remembered. The wildflowers had grown along the path that led down to the pond where she and her father had fished. She remembered her father picking the blossoms and arranging them in her hair. "A crown for my princess," he had said. She had forgotten that. It's no wonder she missed him so much. If he'd lived through her teenage years, he might not have thought she was such a princess.

Emily looked around and noticed she was the only customer in the place: she'd slept through the lunch rush, if there had been one. She pulled out a chair at a window-side table and sat down. From the side wall, two mounted trout gazed blankly in her direction. After sitting quietly for a minute or so, Emily began to wonder if the place closed down in mid-afternoon. Maybe the owners just didn't lock the door, but everyone knew they wouldn't be back until dinner. She was about to get up and leave when a rotund woman came out of the kitchen and saw her. The woman looked her way and seemed surprised to see her.

"Well, hello there," she called. "I didn't hear you come in." The woman slipped a menu under her chubby arm and grabbed a steaming pot of coffee and a pitcher of water and lumbered back toward where Emily sat smiling politely.

"I've been telling Henry to get a bell for that door, but he says I should just keep an eye out instead of having some noisy thing jangling every time someone walks in. Care for coffee?"

"Yes, please," Emily said. The woman set the pitcher of water on the table and handed Emily the menu. "The lunch crowd ate every chicken pie I made this morning, but I've still got beef stew, and we're kind of known for our chili. They say it keeps you cool to eat something spicy in the summer. Where are you from?"

.How did I know she was going to ask me that? Emily thought. "Florida," she told the woman. "Just visiting."

"My son lives in Florida," she said. "Near Orlando. We've been down to visit a couple times, but it's too humid there for me."

She stood looking out at a fishing boat gliding by. Emily realized the woman was waiting to take her order, so she glanced down the menu's listing of sandwiches, the ubiquitous chicken-fried steak that every restaurant in the area seemed to offer, the special note about homemade pies.

"I'll have a cheeseburger," Emily said.

"That comes with french fries and a salad," the woman told her. "What kind of dressing?"

"Blue cheese."

"Got ranch," the woman said. "That okay?"

"Sure," Emily said, handing back the menu.

"You just relax and I'll have your food out in a jiffy," said the woman.

Lumbering, Emily thought, watching the ample-figured woman going back to the kitchen. That's definitely lumbering.

The restaurant door opened and a man came in wearing a fisherman's vest and carrying a pole that he leaned in the corner.

"Hello, Doris," he called to the woman. "Got the coffeepot on?" He seated himself at the counter that curled around the entrance to the kitchen.

"Sure do," her voice rang out. "Help yourself." The man went behind the counter, poured coffee into a mug, and replaced the pot on the warmer.

"Catch any?" she called.

"Nah," the man said. "I got a late start and you know how I fish. Just an excuse to get out of the house."

The man fiddled with his coffee. Emily could hear the sound of hamburger sizzling in the kitchen.

By the time the woman brought Emily's food—salad, burger, and fries at the same time—Emily was starving. The woman retrieved bottles of catsup and mustard from a nearby table. "Can I get you anything else right now, honey?" she asked.

"No," Emily said. "This looks wonderful."

"Well, eat slowly so you can save room for pie. I made coconut cream this morning and there's a big piece left with your name on it." The woman chuckled. Emily felt as if the woman was about to pull out a tissue from her pocket, spit on it, and wipe a smudge from Emily's cheek.

"Well, I'll try," Emily said.

"Now that's all you can ask of a body, isn't it?" said the woman.

As Emily bit into the thick burger, the woman heaved herself onto a stool beside the man drinking coffee. "How about a piece of pie with that?" she asked him.

"Did I hear you say coconut cream? You know I can't resist your coconut cream, Doris."

Emily watched her come back with the pie, pale yellow mounded with thick white topping. Eight hundred calories right there. Two thousand here, she thought, taking another bite of hamburger.

The woman leaned her ample arms on the counter while the man took a big bite of the pie.

"Lord, Doris, you shouldn't do this to us," he said.

"Well, someone in town's got to feed the people, and we sure can't wait for you fishermen to do it." The woman chuckled.

Then another man came in, a big man with short curly gray hair splaying out around his baseball cap. He had a square face, and a wide, blunt nose. When he sat down at the counter, Emily noticed he had big hands like a catcher's mitt. Emily stopped chewing her mouthful of hamburger. The man could have been her father's brother, the resemblance was so strong. In the years since her father's death, she had seen other men who reminded her of him, but this guy was uncanny. Emily couldn't take her eyes off him.

"Hey, Marty," the newcomer said to the man eating pie. "I had the first piece of that pie this morning with breakfast. Soon as it got cool enough to hold together, Doris couldn't keep me out of it," the man said.

Doris came out of the kitchen and around the counter.

"Did you get the box of napkins, honey?" she asked.

"Of course I did, Mother. Think I'd come back here empty-handed?" He stood up and put his thick arm around his wife's neck and gave her a loud kiss on the cheek. Then he poured himself coffee and sat down again between the two.

Emily started to chew again. Her father had no brothers. Not even any cousins that lived around here. But when she looked at the man, she could see her father before illness had left him thin and frail. And to think of it, the woman bore a little resemblance to her mother, too. The calico dress she wore under the white apron could have come right out of her mother's closet. Emily couldn't take her eyes off the two of them.

"I don't know how I ever got along without your cooking, Doris," the man said as he scraped the last bit of pie off his plate. "How long has it been since you all came here?"

"I retired in '78," the man said. "So it's been fourteen years. And we've gotten younger every year, haven't we, Mother?"

She rubbed his back with her chubby hand. "Yes, we have, honey. I told you that'd happen once we got out of those Chicago winds," she said. "I couldn't stand a winter like those again. It robs your strength right out of you. Henry could barely walk when we got here, you know," she went on. "Rheumatism in every joint, and now look at him." She patted him on the back. "He can go to the store for me and buy napkins, and I'll bet he can even carry them in from the truck, too."

The woman chuckled and Henry got up and headed out the door. Emily heard a truck door slam, then Henry came back in carrying a cardboard box and set it on the counter next to Doris.

"Service with a smile." He grinned at his wife. "Got anything else needs servicing?" he said and gave a little pinch to the portion of his wife's rump that hung over the stool.

"Stop that," she said, and swatted at his hand. "Behave yourself. We've got guests."

Henry looked across the restaurant at Emily and tipped his baseball cap. "I'm sorry, ma'am," he said, smiling at Emily. "My wife and I here, we're just so in love we get out of control every now and then."

The three of them laughed and Emily found herself laughing, too. This is how my parents should have been, she thought. A wave of sadness washed over her for a moment while she thought of her mother. She couldn't remember if it had been two or maybe three months since she'd called. She should call her tonight. She would love to hear about Branson. And she'd call Jim, too.

Then Doris was heading her way, carrying a piece of pie.

"I really don't think I can handle that," Emily said. "I'm filled up. The burger was great."

Doris set the pie down on the table and took Emily's salad plate. "Well, you give it a try, on the house. I bet you'll find room for it. And there's no penalty here if you don't clean your plate. Besides, you need a little meat on those bones."

Emily tried the pie. It was delicious. She couldn't believe she was going to eat the whole piece, but she did. Just as she finished the last bite, Doris arrived to replenish her coffee mug.

"Well, now you did just fine, honey," Doris crooned. "I knew you could do it. I just looked at you and saw 'coconut cream pie' in your eyes." The woman leaned toward Emily and said quietly, "Tomorrow's chocolate cream, and it's even better." She straightened. "I grate the chocolate. That's the secret to it. It cooks in better than if you just chuck the whole chunk into the egg yolks. You remember that next time you make it."

Emily had never made a chocolate cream pie, but she assured Doris that she'd remember the tip. She realized how relaxed she felt, safe with people who seemed so normal and everyday. I'm probably relaxed because I ate so much, she thought. She sat for more than half an hour, drinking the coffee as Doris refilled her cup, listening to the three of them talking at the counter about fishing, and Saturday night's Lion's Club benefit, which would be held at the restaurant. Doris talked through the entire menu: ham and beans, her homemade spaghetti sauce, green beans boiled with bacon. Emily couldn't believe her mouth was watering again. After a while, Emily realized that these people hadn't once mentioned Branson. There were no autographed photos of stars on the walls, not even a rack of show brochures in the place. Instead, these people were talking about their neighbors, their friends, a quiet life by the lakeshore.

Finally, Emily waved away the offer of more coffee. "I'm just going to try to stand up," Emily said, patting her tummy.

"Well, you come back and see us again if you have

time while you're here," Doris said. "I bet you're enjoying this weather. I like to sleep with the windows open and pull up the covers as the night cools down. We've been trying to talk our son into coming up here with his family for a visit. Little Jason is almost four, and the baby's just ready to turn two, and I sure miss seeing them. It's a shame when families get all spread out and you can't watch those little ones grow up. It happens so fast." Doris shook her head.

Emily left a two-dollar tip for the six-dollar meal, but she thought of leaving more. And she wished she could come back, although her schedule wasn't going to allow it. For a minute before she got up from the table, she pictured coming in here with Jim for dinner on a Sunday afternoon, sitting at this table as the sun set over the lake. And then just for a flash, she pictured a little girl seated with them, a tyke of about three, carefully opening a package of crackers while Mom and Dad held hands.

Gee-eeze, Emily thought, stirring out of her reverie. What was in that pie?

When she had paid, she said goodbye to Doris and waved to the two men at the counter.

"Good luck. Have a nice visit," both called. "Come back Saturday night."

Outside, Emily couldn't face getting back in her car quite yet. She strolled along the lakefront sidewalk and watched the people fishing. No one was casting or reeling in. They were just leaning against the dock railing, or sitting on the banks, their lines floating out toward the center of the narrow lake. It might have been a still life painting.

Emily sat down on a bench. A little girl of about six, dressed in red shorts and a striped T-shirt, was passing out orange corn curls to a flock of Canadian geese. She dipped her short arm into the bag and came out with a handful, then cautiously held the long crunchy snacks out to the geese one at a time. The geese were polite, approaching one by one to snatch a corn curl from the girl's hand. Each time, she squealed and laughed. Emily found herself laughing aloud watching the flock of geese waddling around with what looked like orange cigar butts protruding from their mouths. The little girl lost interest in the game before the geese, who followed her in single file as she skipped up the bank toward one of the resort cabins.

When Emily looked back at the lakefront, she could have sworn none of the fishermen had moved a muscle.

★ *14* ★

Emily had wasted the entire day. She'd driven around on the two-lane roads for hours, listening to Paul Simon and Jimmy Buffett tapes. She'd stopped at a roadside produce stand and bought a dark green acorn squash and some green beans that the woman had picked that morning, and two big tomatoes, still warm from the vine. If she had an appetite that evening after the big lunch, some vegetables would be nice. She pictured the squash, steaming in the oven with a pool of butter melting in each half.

And she pictured Fluffy enjoying her tuna fish. She was seriously thinking of taking the kitten home with her. It was obvious she was a stray, and now she had come to depend on Emily. It wasn't that she could ever replace Shakespeare. But she liked having a cat at home with her in the evenings. She'd been thinking about getting another one for some time. This seemed like fate: a kind of living souvenir from Branson.

She also had stopped at two flea markets, wandered through rooms of old glassware and cooking pots, old tools and horse bridles, dolls and scruffy teddy bears that had seen a lot of love. In one of the shops, Emily bought a pair of glass candleholders for ten dollars. They were

heavy pressed glass, nothing special, except that they reminded her of a pair of candlesticks her mother used to
have on the sideboard in their little Blue Eye home. She
never remembered her mother lighting the red tapers
they held, and she thought that when she got home, she'd
take them to her mother along with new candles, and
she'd light the candles. Maybe she'd take the fixings for
Chinese food when she went to see her. First she thought
of how the gesture would please her mother. Then she
realized she, too, was looking forward to it.

When Emily returned to her cabin, it was nearly dark,
and Fluffy was waiting by her door. They shared a late dinner of fresh vegetables and tuna fish and went to sleep together, curled up and content.

On Friday morning Emily awoke and realized it was her
last day in the Ozarks. She thought of Doris baking her
chocolate pies and regretted she wouldn't see her again.
Emily was excited about the show and the stars she would
meet today. The Hacketts and Stella Love and Cowboy
Robert seemed like characters in a bad movie she'd seen.
Soon, she vowed, she'd forget that plot.

The day would be a busy one. She had to get to the
theater early to be able to interview the big stars. She was
hoping for short interviews with Glen Campbell and
Louise Mandrell. She'd done her homework and had a list
of questions she would ask each one, about their work,
their hits, their special interests, and most importantly,
their view of the Branson scene. She also had prepared
herself to interview Johnny Cash. He was to fly in that afternoon, but the arrangements still weren't completely con-
firmed. She hoped he would be there. She was still a bit
star-struck, and Cash certainly qualified for "legend" sta-
tus.

With a final snuggle, she set Fluffy outside the cabin

door and headed for the shower. As she dried off, she laid out the black cocktail dress she'd brought to wear that night. It seemed so tame and proper. She took her faux pearl necklace out of the jewelry case and resolved to stop on the way into town for a quick look to see if she could find a necklace and earrings that were a little more flashy.

For the afternoon interviews, Emily wore her white cotton dress and beige blazer. She gathered up her reporter's notebook and a file of information on tonight's show, and headed for town.

When she pulled up behind Lyle's theater, two black limousines were parked beside the entrance. Inside the theater, there was still a lot of activity, but somehow things seemed a little more calm. From the wings, Emily could see the stage set that had been merely a wooden framework a couple of days ago. Now the curving stairway was white, glittering with silver bows and sprays of silver roses. A white grand piano at the bottom of the stairs held a Liberace candelabra. Big gold-painted stars provided the backdrop and strings of smaller stars sparkled with the sway of the curtains. White wicker baskets on either side of the stage held arrangements of long-stemmed red roses. Even from the side where Emily could see unpainted two-by-fours bracing the set, it was spectacular. And the lucky audience would see only the illusion, not the timbers and wires that held it all together.

Onstage, BoxCar Willie was chatting with some of the stagehands, demonstrating his famous train whistle, done without a whistle in his mouth. Emily saw him open his mouth to demonstrate to the onlookers that nothing was hidden. Then she heard what sounded like the lonesome wail of an old steam engine.

Emily needed to find Lyle. He would introduce her to the stars she needed to interview. And he was to have a ticket for her in the front section for the show. Emily

164

headed for his dressing room. There were a lot of people backstage who all seemed to be going somewhere. The hallway was crowded, and she stayed close to the wall. She could see the door to Lyle's dressing room was slightly ajar, and as she was about to knock, she heard John Hackett's unmistakable rasping voice.

"Then you just seat them somewhere else, Lyle," Hackett said. "I want those three seats. I told Heather we'd be in the front row, so that's where we'll be."

"They're friends of Johnny Cash's," Lyle said. "I can't seat them in the back row, and those are the only seats I've got left. Can't you and your little honey just stand backstage? She'd be thrilled with that, wouldn't she?"

"Let Johnny's freeloading friends stand backstage," Hackett said. "Let's not forget who put this show together, ol' boy."

"Well, let's not forget whose theater this is, either," came Lyle's voice. Emily heard a scuffle and a grunt, the sound of something hitting a wall. The people hurrying along the hallway seemed oblivious to Emily and to the sounds coming from the dressing room, so she leaned forward in order to see through the three-inch space of the open door. Reflected in one of the wall mirrors, John Hackett had Lyle pinned against the opposite wall. His left hand was clutching Lyle's throat and his right hand was raised in a fist. Before Emily could move, Hackett lowered his fist and grabbed Lyle's shirtfront with both hands. Lyle's face was beet-red.

"Listen, you son of a bitch," Hackett was saying in Lyle's face, "I haven't forgotten anything. I haven't forgotten the juicy little videotape I've got of you porking the ever lovely Jennifer, the ever *seventeen* Jennifer. Let's not forget what would happen to your reputation and your theater if that gets sent to a TV station."

Emily saw sweat running down Lyle's red face. Hackett let go of his shirt, but kept Lyle pressed against the wall. "You get me those tickets. I don't care what you do with those other people, but I will have those front seats or you'll become the King of Skin Flicks. Do we understand each other?" Hackett asked while he straightened Lyle's collar.

Lyle pushed away from the other man. He was gasping for breath.

"I've had enough of you, Hackett," Lyle said. "You've pushed me too far for too long."

In a flash, Hackett had Lyle pinned against the wall again. Lyle's mouth was open. His eyes bulged. Emily looked to see if anyone was around who could come to Lyle's aid. She didn't know what to do.

"You don't know what it's like to be pushed by me," Hackett said in a voice barely audible to Emily. She couldn't hear what else he said because just then two young men walked past her and into the open dressing room. They were each carrying a cardboard box and set them on the dressing table before they looked around and noticed John and Lyle, who were standing apart, both breathing heavily.

"These are the trophies," one of the young men told Lyle. "Do you want them here or should we take them out to the stage?"

"Leave them here," Lyle said, trying to catch his breath. "I need to take a look at them first."

The two left and Emily seized the opportunity to knock on the door. "Lyle, it's Emily," she said, walking into the room.

"It's the press, Mr. Malone," said Hackett with an evil grin. "What timing. Anything you want to say to the press?"

Lyle looked at Hackett. "I'll leave the tickets in the box office," Lyle said.

166

"Thank you," Hackett said. He turned to leave and walked up to stand very close to Emily. She could feel his breath and smell his . . . It was English Leather she had smelled in her cabin Wednesday. It wasn't the maid's disinfectant. He was in the cabin, she realized with horror. He searched my room. And he took the Kleenex out of the peephole. Her neck tingled and she took a step backward.

"Enjoy the show," Hackett said. "I'll see you tonight." Then he was gone. Lyle and Emily stared at each other. Lyle wiped his face and sat down, motioning for Emily to do the same. The only sound was Lyle's labored breathing.

"How much did you hear?" he wheezed.

"Enough to know he's got a tight grip on you," Emily said softly. "Why'd you let him get away with that, Lyle? Surely your fans love you enough to forgive your being human. We all make mistakes."

"Not like this, Emily." Lyle got up and closed the dressing-room door. "They wouldn't forgive this." Lyle took a drink from a bottle of spring water. "She was seventeen, Emily. The girl was only seventeen. It's over the legal age limit in Missouri, but she was still young enough to have been my granddaughter. I knew she was young, but I figured her to be in her twenties."

He looked at her and shook his head. "No matter how old she was, it wasn't right. It happened two years ago, a year after I lost my wife. I was depressed, and I was drinking too much. It was out on Hackett's boat. He fixed it all up. He fixed up the video camera he's got installed in that downstairs cabin too, but of course I didn't find out about the camera until later when he started wanting favors. No, Emily. My fans wouldn't forgive me. I can't forgive myself."

"But what are you going to do? You can't just let him go on running your life like this," Emily said. "That's why you were going to let Stella Love perform on the show to-night, isn't it?"

"Yes," Lyle said. "It sure wasn't to showcase her talent. And now I've got Monica running around like a wounded bear because I didn't schedule her for that spot. I don't know what I'm going to do with Hackett."

Lyle sat slumped in the chair. He looked about a hundred years old. Emily went over to him and took his hand in both of hers.

"You're a good man, Lyle. People know that. We all make mistakes," Emily told him. But she knew he was right. A lot of his fans would be too shocked to think about forgiveness. She stood next to him holding his hand and they didn't talk for a minute.

"What's the matter with John's eye?" Emily finally asked. "It makes him look so weird."

"He is weird," Lyle said. "It happened years ago. He thinks he can do anything, so he was changing the headlamp in his car. A spring came out and hit him right in the eye. Left him blind in that eye. Too bad it didn't kill him."

"I think he might have killed Stella," Emily said. "I went upstairs after we talked in the library, and I overheard them fighting. She threatened to tell everyone he was impotent."

"Impotent! Is that a fact? I hadn't thought John was capable of killing someone. Irene's been my prime suspect. She's so much stronger than he is, and smarter. But something like that could have driven him to do anything. Does anyone know you were eavesdropping?"

"No, but I did tell the sheriff I'd heard a rumor that Stella was blackmailing John."

"You told Turner? I'm sure the first thing he did was to warn Irene, and Irene probably told John. Young lady, you better be careful where you stand for the next few hours. Watch your back, and get out of here as soon as you can. It's possible it really was an accident. But if Stella was threatening to reveal that he's not a man anymore, John might have gone crazy. He's a proud man who never wanted to admit his age. That's why he keeps all the young beauties around. He might have killed her to preserve his image of his own youth."

"Just like Porphyria's Lover."

"What's that?"

"Oh, just a poem about a man who kills his lover so that she'll never age."

"Well, I'm no detective, and neither are you. Just be careful, dear. And stay away from John."

Lyle patted her hand. Then he stood up and took a deep breath. "Come on, lady. We got a show to put on. Let's go see if anyone else famous is here yet." He grinned at her with a smile that erased years from his face.

Two doors down the hall, Lyle tapped on a dressing room. A young woman opened the door.

"Hi, Lyle," she said.

"Hi, there," he said. "Is Louise busy? I've got someone I want her to meet."

"I'm never too busy for a friend of yours," said a sultry voice from inside the dressing room. Louise Mandrell looked stunning in a black workout leotard. She was tiny, and obviously kept herself in good shape. Emily's homework had told her she and Louise were the same age, but Emily felt like a fat, lumpy old woman beside the svelte star. She was sure no one would catch Louise wolfing down coconut cream pie. It wasn't just the trim body that was attractive. Louise had a beautiful shiny mane of dark brown hair that moved when she moved. Definitely no need for a wig in this room, Emily thought.

"This is Emily Stone," Lyle said. "She's the travel writer for the *Tampa Tribune* and she's going to write a nice story about the show tonight. Can you spare her a few minutes?"

Louise and Emily shook hands.

"A few. For you, Lyle," Louise said. "Let's sit down."

As Emily had found sometimes in other interviews with entertainers, it only took a couple of questions to get them started talking. All you had to do was establish that you'd done your homework, that you hadn't blundered in cold not knowing the person's background, and that you were polite and not confrontational. Emily asked Louise about the Christmas show she was planning to do with her sisters. She asked Louise what she thought of her stint in Branson. That was all it took. With few interruptions from Emily, Louise talked for twenty minutes about the blessing she got from the Lord when He sent her to Branson, how wonderful it was to be close to the audiences, how great the cast of dancers were. Emily took notes, and nodded and smiled, but she was disappointed. This sounded like an interview Louise must have given a hundred times. It sounded staged, rehearsed. Emily knew it was hopeless, that nothing spontaneous was likely to happen. She had the feeling that if she challenged anything the star was saying, or asked any questions for which there wasn't a ready answer, Emily would be ushered back into the hallway. But Louise was as perky offstage as she seemed onstage, and that was what Emily would include in her story. And she'd mention the family portrait that sat on Louise's dressing table next to a large bouquet of pink roses. The open closet that ran the length of the dressing room was hung with sequined gowns, long and short, and Emily saw sparkles of red, blue, green. She thought of the colorful cabins at Rocky Shores.

Then Louise excused herself and Emily was back in the busy hallway. A man hurried by, talking into a portable phone. "He's about five minutes out," he said. "He'll be landing in five minutes. Get security out back. Everyone," he said.

That must be Johnny Cash about to arrive, Emily thought. Just then Lyle came out of his dressing room, wearing a rhinestone-studded bolo and bead-trimmed jacket over his overalls.

"Come on," he said to Emily. "Johnny's about to land. I'll try to get him to talk to you, but he might be tired."

Lyle looked excited, undaunted by his dispute with the unpleasant Mr. Hackett. Emily was excited, too. Short of interviewing Willie Nelson—an experience that had left her daydreaming about life on the road for days—this was the interview of a lifetime.

The parking lot behind the theater had been roped off with yellow plastic tape, and at least a dozen uniformed theater employees were cautioning a growing crowd to stay out of the perimeter. In the distance, Emily could hear the *whap-whap* of a helicopter approaching. As the helicopter came within sight, the size of the crowd grew until two or three hundred people were lining the square marked off for the arrival.

"Hello, Lyle," some shouted when he walked out of the theater. "We love you."

Lyle waved at the crowd and smiled at Emily. "I wouldn't do anything in the world to hurt those people," he said quietly.

With a gust of wind from the rotors, the helicopter landed. From inside the aircraft, two people came out and turned to help the black-clad man down the steps. A cheer came up from the crowd as Johnny Cash stopped on the steps to wave. Then he headed toward Lyle and Emily.

"Hello, John." Lyle hugged the big man.

"Hello, Lyle."

Emily had wondered if Cash's speaking voice in person would be as sonorous and impressive as his singing voice. She wasn't disappointed. If she'd been in an unlighted room, she would have recognized his voice. Lyle pointed toward Emily.

"John, I want you to meet my friend Emily Stone.

171

She's a journalist from Florida. If you feel up to it, Emily would like to do a short interview."

"That'd be fine," the famous voice said. "Pleasure to meet you." He held out his hand to Emily.

I'm shaking hands with Johnny Cash, she thought. I'm going to speak. Come on, voice.

"Hello," was all that came out. Get a grip, she told herself. It won't be much of an interview if I can't talk.

Surrounded by a cluster of security guards, Emily walked with Lyle and Johnny back into the building while the crowd cheered them on. Inside, Lyle ushered Cash into an unoccupied dressing room. His two attendants came in carrying a large black case and garment bags.

"Thank you, Lyle," Cash said. "Give me about ten minutes and come back," he said to Emily, who stood in the doorway.

"What's the first thing you'd need to do after an hour in a helicopter?" Lyle said to Emily and chuckled as he closed the door.

"You have a good interview and I'll see you later," he said. Then he gave Emily a hug and held her tight for a moment before he turned to go to his own dressing room.

Emily leaned against the wall and opened her notebook to review the questions she'd jotted down to ask Johnny Cash. She could hear her heart pounding. Ten minutes later, Emily took several deep breaths and knocked on the door.

"Are you ready?" Johnny Cash asked when he opened the door. He motioned for her to come in, pointed at a chair, and sat down on the black leather couch.

"I kind of blend into this, don't I?" he said, gesturing toward his black shirt, black pants, and black boots. His smile was kind and genuine. He's trying to put me at ease, she realized. This is a really nice man.

Emily was glad to see that he didn't try to color the gray that streaked his hair. He looked older than she thought he would. Deep lines around his eyes and mouth showed that he'd lived a full and maybe even reckless life sometimes. But he still looked robust, and there was a lively sparkle in his dark eyes. There were so many questions this man must have been asked a million times. She was not going to ask the obvious, she had promised herself.

"How's June?" she began, and immediately thought perhaps she'd made a mistake. She hadn't asked Johnny how he was. She should have done that first. But it didn't seem to make any difference.

"She's fine. I left her home in Nashville because this was just a one-day trip. You know, she's an antiques hunter and if I brought her over here where you all have all these little shops I might have trouble getting her home," Cash said. He sat and looked at Emily and waited for the next question.

"Why did you decide to do this show in Branson?" Emily asked. This wasn't going to be one of those easy interviews where they do all the talking, she thought.

But she was wrong. Once Cash started talking about Branson, he got going, talking about the roots of country music, how he felt privileged to work with the Carter Family, and he talked about his daughter Roseanne's career and his son who was playing with his band now. After a few minutes, he stood up and went to the dressing-room fridge.

"Let's see what they left me," he said. "Would you like something?" Emily declined, thinking that she could use a stiff martini right now. What he picked from the stock of soft drinks and fruit juices was a bottle of spring water. As he turned to come back to the couch, Emily saw him look in the mirror. She wondered how his view of himself differed from what she saw as she looked at a venerable legend.

So she asked. Every once in a while, Emily had to admit she came up with a brilliant spur-of-the-moment question. Cash thought about it for a minute. He looked at himself in the mirror again. Emily's pen was poised.

"Well, I just see the person I've always seen," he said. "Other people call me a legend. I don't really know what that means, but I've been called a lot of things and that's probably one of the nicest."

All right, thought Emily. Now that's a quote. I bet he's never said that in just that way to anyone else.

She had been with Cash for about fifteen minutes. He was talking about a recent concert tour he'd done in Europe when Lyle poked his head through the door.

"I hate to disturb you, but if you're about finished we need John onstage to do a walk-through of his presentation tonight," Lyle said.

Emily shook hands with the big man in black, and thanked Lyle for his help.

"See you later," she said. "Break a leg."

Emily looked at her watch. It was nearly five. If she was going to shop for jewelry, get home and change, and get back for the show at eight P.M., she'd have to hurry. She knew the traffic into town tonight would be murder.

A few blocks from the theater, Emily saw a small dress shop. A sign in the window read Clearance Sale—Big Bargains. That was just what she needed. Whatever she bought for tonight she'd most likely never wear again.

Inside, she quickly picked out a mid-length necklace of gold chains with large crystal beads dangling at irregular intervals and a matched pair of earrings. The sale price came to twenty-five dollars. Emily strutted out, pleased with her purchase, anticipating her glamorous appearance that evening when she would undoubtedly meet several other entertainers.

174

Emily headed straight for her cabin. Time for a quick shower, a quick job with the curling iron—or maybe she'd put her hair up for the evening. She was wondering if she'd remembered to pack hairpins when she pulled up to the cabin. She was pleased to see the white figure of Fluffy waiting on the front porch.

"Hi, Fluff," Emily called as she got out of the car and reached back in for her shopping bag. "Ready for more tuna?"

She walked toward the porch. Fluffy didn't move. Emily's eyes widened in horror and she slapped her hand over her mouth to hold back a scream. The small kitten lay dead on its side in a pool of blood, its eyes rolled back to reveal only blank white orbs. Protruding upright from the side of the kitten's soft belly, a violin bow pointed toward the sky.

15

Emily stared at the cat and took several steps backward. She couldn't move. Finally she backed away several additional steps, her hand still over her mouth. Suddenly she was afraid as the full realization of what she was seeing hit her. She ran back to her car and got in and locked the door. She crouched as if expecting bullets to shatter the window glass at any moment. She looked in all directions, but there was no one in sight. There were no other cars at nearby cabins, no one stirring except a fishing boat trolling past on the lake.

Then the tears came, tears of pain at the injustice of the poor kitten's death and rage at the monster who could have committed such an act. It's not a random act, she thought. It's aimed at me, to warn me, like the message on my car. I should have gotten out of here then.

Emily started the car and drove back to the highway where she dialed the sheriff's department from a phone booth at a gas station. It was after six P.M. on a Friday and Emily half expected no one would answer the phone.

"Sheriff's Department," a woman said, sounding as if she were angry to be catching the night shift on a Friday.

"Hi. This is Emily Stone. Is the sheriff still there?"

"No. He's gone home. Can I help you?"

"Yes. I'm a reporter from the *Tampa Tribune* and I'm in town doing a story about Branson. I need you to send someone out right away to the Bitterroot Resort where I'm staying." Emily stopped, not knowing exactly how to put the next part of what she was going to tell this disinterested woman.

"Someone is trying to terrorize me," Emily said. "I've had other threats earlier this week that I reported to Sheriff Turner, and now they've killed a kitten and left it on my doorstep."

"Well, ma'am, maybe the kitten just died there by accident. Sometimes stray kittens just up and die if they haven't been raised right," the woman said.

"No," Emily said. "This was no accident. It was . . . stabbed to death . . ." Emily took a deep breath before she said, "With a violin bow."

There was a momentary silence on the other end of the line. "Stabbed with a violin bow?" the woman asked. "A fiddle bow?"

"That's right. It was a kitten I've been taking care of the past few days. I think someone knew that I'd been friendly with the kitten. Someone's warning me to leave town. Can an officer come out right away?"

"Well, maybe you should just take the warning and leave town, ma'am," the woman suggested. "I know a dead cat on my porch would sure put the skids to my vacation."

Emily was sick of this. She raised her voice. "Look. I'm not here on vacation. I'm a working reporter and I'm here investigating a murder. How fast can someone get out here?"

The firm declaration seemed to have the desired effect.

"I'll get a deputy out there," the woman said. "What cabin are you in?"

Emily drove back to the turnoff to the resort and parked by the side of the road to wait. After ten minutes, Emily stopped trembling. She got out of the car and paced around it. After twenty minutes had passed, she was angry and about to drive back to the phone booth when a deputy's car turned down the road. Emily followed it and pulled in at her cabin. The uniformed deputy was squatting by the front porch, looking at the kitten and shaking his head.

"That's a bad thing, ma'am," he said, pulling out a notebook from his breast pocket. "Do you have any idea who did this?" He tapped the fiddle bow with the tip of his pen.

"No," Emily said. "Obviously, it's someone who wants me to leave town, which is exactly what I'm going to do."

"Is this yours?" the deputy asked, tapping the bow again. Emily cringed at the hollow sound.

"No," she said. "Why?"

"Well, it's too small to be a real fiddle bow," he said. "It's like a toy or something. I thought maybe you knew what it was."

The image came to mind immediately. Lyle playing with the miniature fiddle in the Hacketts' library. Emily could hear the shriek the bow had made against the strings.

"I saw a small violin with a bow like that last week at John Hackett's house," Emily told the young deputy.

"Did you? I guess they sell these in souvenir shops."

"But I think Hackett did this. I think he searched my cabin, and he knows I suspect he killed Stella Love at his party last week."

"She fell off the balcony, didn't she?"

"He pushed her. Just tell Sheriff Turner what's happened. And someone needs to go to the Hacketts' and see if the violin bow is missing."

"Well, we'll sure investigate this," he said, sounding unconvinced.

"Also," Emily went on. "There's been a man staying in this cabin next door, and I think it might be someone you're looking for. Turner knows about him. I'm sure he's the man who was stalking Stella. He told me his name was Robert Simmons, but I think he's really Robert Smith. He drives a black pickup truck from Texas."

"Oh, right, Smith," the deputy said. "We picked him up last night, headed out of town in that pickup. We haven't filed charges, but we're questioning him."

Emily thought of Robert in a cell. Suddenly she was glad she hadn't been responsible for him getting caught.

"Well, ma'am," the deputy said, "I'll make a report to the sheriff on this. We could try to get prints off this bow"—he tapped it again—"but it's a long shot. This was probably just a sick prank of some kind." He stood up and turned to her. "When were you planning to leave town?" he asked.

Not fast enough to suit you, I bet, Emily thought. "Another nutty tourist," she could hear him telling the sheriff over donuts and coffee.

"If you'll remove the cat," Emily said, "I'll pack right now. I have to attend the awards show tonight and I'll be out of town as soon as it's over."

Emily thought about the hour-long drive to Springfield where her plane would leave at noon tomorrow. Surely she could find a motel there. If not, she'd sleep in the car tonight. But she wouldn't come back here anymore.

The deputy retrieved a black plastic garbage bag from his car. He lifted the kitten by the embedded violin bow. The bow didn't pull out of the body and Emily looked away as the deputy deposited his find in the garbage bag.

The deputy set the bag next to his car. "Better let me take a look inside," he said. Emily handed him her key and stood outside. She looked at the trash bag and thought about the kitten. She would have taken Fluffy home tomorrow. Tears came to Emily's eyes.

"I don't see anything wrong in there," he said when he came out. "You want to take a look?"

The deputy led the way back into the cabin. A slight scent of English Leather lingered in the air, but nothing looked awry. Emily opened a couple of drawers as though she were checking to see if there'd been a theft. She opened the nightstand drawer while the deputy's back was turned. The gun lay undisturbed on the towel.

I wish I'd seen him do it, she thought with rage.

"Well, I'll take this back to the office," the deputy said. "If you want, I'll wait while you pack."

"No," Emily said. She still had to shower and dress for the show as well as pack, and she had barely enough time as it was. "I don't think anyone will come back now. I think they've made their point."

After the deputy left, Emily locked the door. She took a wooden chair from the kitchen table and wedged the back of the door under the knob. She'd always seen that done in movies and she wasn't sure how effective it might be against a dedicated intruder, but at least she'd hear if someone were trying to get in. Emily decided against a shower. Too many images of killers sneaking up to shower curtains came to mind. As she let the bathwater run, Emily checked to see that the bedroom peephole was still securely plugged. She peeked out each curtained window, surveying three views of the resort. A man and two young boys were down by the lakefront, skimming stones in the reddish glow of the setting sun. No one else was in sight.

Emily turned off the bathwater and laid the gun beside the tub. Let him come back, she thought. The warm bath was not relaxing.

Emily packed her suitcase, put her notes in her briefcase, and did a quick cleanup of dishes she'd left in the sink from last night's vegetable dinner. She left two cans of tuna fish in a cupboard. In her jogging suit, she moved the chair out of the way of the door. On the step outside, the puddle of blood had dried and was now a dark red stain. One good rain and there wouldn't be a trace of anything. She carried the bags to the car. From the briefcase, she took the small pistol and put it in the glove compartment.

Then she put on the black dress and the sparkling jewelry. She looked in the mirror; while she was pleased with the look, she felt none of her earlier enthusiasm. She just wanted to get the job done and get out of here.

She took a last look around the cabin, checking drawers and the bathroom cupboard to make sure she had left nothing. Then she spied the tissue plugging the peephole in the bedroom wall. Emily pulled a black Sharpie felt-tipped pen out of her purse. She drew an arrow pointing to the peephole on the pale blue painted wall. Next to the arrow, in big letters, she scrawled, "Beware. Secret peephole."

That might get her a bill from the management, but maybe they'd plug the holes now. Then she shut the cabin door, stepped around the smear of dried blood, and drove away from the Bitterroot toward the glitter of the neon strip.

16

The headlights of cars lined up in both directions coming into the theater's parking lot looked like a diamond necklace. Emily waited in the traffic for fifteen minutes, edging her way toward the theater. She felt miserable, and the traffic annoyed her. In her mind, eyes swirled like a cyclone funnel—the white, blank stare of the kitten, John Hackett's empty black pupil, Stella staring at the sky. A few more hours and she'd be gone.

She was almost at the theater's parking lot. Women in sparkling gowns and men in tuxedos streamed toward the theater. In front, the beams from two giant searchlights mounted on truck beds sent spiraled patterns into the night sky. Lyle Malone's country tunes blared from speakers outside the theater and at intervals throughout the parking lot.

The parking place to which Emily was directed by a row of uniformed attendants waving flashlights was the length of a football field from the theater. Because many of the theaters in Branson had been built at the top of the ridge that ran through town, parking lots were notably sloped, and as Emily trudged up the hill, she heard, and silently sympathized with, complaints from several women about the condition of their feet in their high-heeled shoes.

Inside, the lobby was crowded. Waiters wearing tuxedo shirts and black slacks edged their way between people, holding aloft silver trays with glasses of champagne and flavored sparkling waters. The bubbling pastel drinks gleamed with reflections of the giant crystal chandeliers overhead. Scattered through the crowd of local leaders, business people, and visiting dignitaries from the country-music industry, were a handful of tourists who had been able to get tickets, recognizable by their casual dress and their scrutiny of the other guests.

But Emily knew the stars weren't out there in the crowd. They would be brought in through the stage door and quietly ushered to their seats after the houselights dimmed. During the show, the stars in the audience would be introduced and would stand and wave as a spotlight shone on them, but that was as close as the fans would get tonight. Emily was seated in the section reserved for the stars, their families, and locals like the mayor and town council members, people who were unimpressed by the entertainers they saw from time to time at the grocery store or on the golf course. To them, a star was just another person and they wouldn't be pressing them for handshakes and autographs.

"The only star I'd pester is Richard Gere," Emily had told Lyle.

"Well, you can relax because he turned down his invitation," Lyle joked.

The auditorium hadn't been opened yet for seating, and Emily made her way through the crowd to a guard who looked at the "All Access" press pass hung around her neck and opened the door for her. The three-thousand-seat theater, decorated in deep maroon with gold trim, was softly lit by crystal lights mounted along the walls and chandeliers overhead. Several small groups of female ushers stood talking, waiting for the rush that would soon come. From behind the lowered maroon velvet curtain, Emily heard the sound of someone plucking a fiddle and the whine of a steel guitar tuning up. Emily walked down the long aisle to the stage door and went through to a narrow hallway that led to the backstage area. Ahead of her, she could hear the soft buzz of conversation from stagehands, dressers, and other staff standing by for the opening number. Emily felt a stab of excitement like a rush of adrenaline.

The only door off the hallway was the theater manager's office. A table lamp was on, and as Emily neared the door, she could see the shadow of a couple standing together apparently locked in an embrace. Emily instinctively halted, wondering if Hackett was auditioning a new starlet. In the hushed hallway, she heard the sucking sounds of wet lips, then a woman's sigh. Emily backstepped silently in the carpeted hall until she was at the backstage door.

"I'd better go," she heard the woman say. Then Monica came out of the office. Monica was looking down at her red satin dress, straightening the skirt, and didn't look toward where Emily stood, frozen, her hand on the doorknob. In a moment, Monica disappeared around the corner that led to the dressing rooms. Emily stayed put, watching the office door.

Robert Simmons stopped dead in his tracks when he walked out of the office and saw Emily standing by the door, but it took only a moment for him to regain his composure.

"Hello, Emily," he said. He didn't smile as he walked toward her. "Guess you didn't expect to see me tonight. Sorry I had to miss our date last night. I wonder if you showed up at Rocky's?" He paused, but Emily didn't say anything.

"They let me out of jail this afternoon because they

found no reason to keep me," he said evenly. "They don't think I killed Stella. I wonder who told the sheriff I was in Branson? Who do you think did that?" Simmons asked.

Emily said nothing. Simmons reached for the doorknob and Emily pulled back her hand. Simmons smiled at her and shook his head. "Too bad you're such a nervous lady, sugarcane," he said and gave her chin a pinch. "We could have had some fun."

Then he opened the door and walked through. He didn't look back as the door slowly closed. Emily leaned against the wall, listening to her heart pounding. Robert and Monica? she thought. That's got to be the topper. Nothing else can happen now.

Slowly, Emily walked down the hall toward the dressing rooms. She wanted to see Lyle. She didn't want to see Monica, and she certainly didn't want to see Hackett. But there he was, standing in the wings near the side curtains of the stage, smoking a cigarette.

"Well, we meet again," he said when he saw her.

"Hello, Mr. Hackett," Emily said. She kept walking, intending to pass him without stopping, but he took a step in front of her.

"How's your story about Branson coming along?" he asked, smiling. "Finding plenty of material?"

"Yes," Emily said coolly. "I think everyone will be pleased with my article." She tried to sidestep him, but he stepped in front of her and she had to stop or touch him; it was as though a cobra were in her path.

"Well, I for one am looking forward to reading it," he said slowly, grinning, "especially since I'm a friend of the writer's." Hackett put his hand on top of Emily's shoulder. He gripped her firmly and she didn't move, but every muscle tensed and she shifted her weight onto one foot, ready to rocket her right knee to his groin if he made one more move. Her mind filled with the image of the dead kitten.

185

"You know, I have some friends in Tampa," he said quietly. "I'll tell them to keep an eye out for your byline. You leaving for home tomorrow?" He removed his hand from her shoulder and stepped on the cigarette butt he had dropped on the carpeting.

"Tonight," she said, looking straight into his gaping pupil. "Right after the show. Would you excuse me?"

"Certainly. It's been a pleasure, ma'am," he said, bowing slightly and stepping to the side.

Emily didn't look back, but felt certain his eyes were on her back. She wanted to run to find Lyle, but as she hurried past the edge of the backdrop curtain, Emily saw Sheriff Turner standing by himself, watching the activity backstage. He didn't smile when he saw her approaching. Emily didn't care. I'll kick him in the balls too if need be.

"Hello, Sheriff Turner," she said before he opened his mouth. "Did you hear about my kitten?"

"Yes, ma'am. It's a shame."

"Did you search the Hacketts' house for that miniature violin?"

"No. We haven't done that."

"Sheriff, I'm certain he did it. And certain he pushed Stella," Emily said in a low voice. She moved a step closer to him, away from the backdrop curtain that rippled behind her. "I overheard Stella threaten him at the party. It wasn't just a rumor. And I'd be willing to testify to that." Emily realized that would mean coming back to Branson, but maybe that wouldn't be so bad if Hackett was locked up.

"I'm leaving for Springfield right after the show, but I'll call you in the morning before my plane leaves."

The sheriff hesitated for a moment. "I've got an early tee time in the morning, but I'll be going by the office about nine-thirty. You can reach me then." He didn't smile, but neither did he demean her with his sarcastic "ma'am." And Emily thought she saw a gleam of interest in his eyes. Maybe he had finally seen a way to prosecute Hackett.

"Thank you," Emily said coldly, and walked away toward Lyle's dressing room.

A glance at her watch showed her it was ten minutes until the show began. From the scurry of activity backstage, Emily decided she'd better forgo seeing Lyle now. He'd be too busy and she might be unwelcome. She didn't need another negative encounter with anyone right now, so she turned and, seeing the hallway leading to the auditorium door empty, she quickly walked, almost bolted, past the stage, the office, and with relief, out into the auditorium, now nearly filled with people.

Emily handed her ticket to an usher who led her to a seat in the sixth row on the center aisle. Emily recognized some of the people sitting around her from the Hacketts' parties. In the front row, she saw the back of John Hackett's head. Irene sat on his left. On his right was a young blond beauty that Emily hadn't seen before. As she watched, she saw Irene lean over and say something to John, then leave her seat and walk toward Emily.

"Hello, Irene," Emily said, wondering what was about to happen. Emily tensed up. "What a beautiful dress."

"Thank you, Emily," Irene said. She was wearing a short rose silk dress and the color flattered her. In fact, she really did look lovely.

"I just wanted to tell you something," Irene said, squatting in the aisle beside Emily's seat. "I know it probably won't sound like much to you, but I'm so proud of it. I got a letter today from the editor of *The Saturday Press* and they accepted one of my poems for publication. It's not the most prestigious journal, but they take a special interest in women writers over the age of forty. I really appreciated your kind words about my poetry last week, Emily, so I wanted to tell you."

Irene couldn't have suppressed her smile by order of God. "I just can't describe how good I felt when I read the acceptance letter. I can't remember anything making me feel that good, and I want to write all the time now. I'd like to send you a copy of the journal when it comes out, if that'd be all right?"

"Of course," Emily said. "I'd love to see it, and I'll expect copies of future poems you have published too, and an autographed copy of your first book."

Irene continued grinning ear to ear. "Well, I'm not thinking about anything like that," she said without much conviction. "But I'll keep trying."

"You have to dream big, Irene," Emily said. "You can do whatever you set your mind to."

The houselights dimmed. "Thank you, Emily, for your encouragement," Irene said and returned to her seat.

Good for you, Emily thought. I wonder how much she'll like me when I help put her husband away.

Then the band started, the audience began applauding, and the curtain rose. The stage looked beautiful and Emily forgot about all the wires and trappings she'd seen in the days before. There were Monica and two other backup singers, all smiles and sparkles. And then Lyle came out. When he started to sing, Emily realized that he too had been transformed. Wrinkles and worries didn't show in the spotlight's glow.

For the next hour and a half, Emily was transfixed by the music and the charisma of the enthusiastic stars. She swore Johnny Cash looked twenty years younger onstage than he had when Emily had talked with him only hours earlier. And when he began to sing after the enthusiastic standing ovation, Emily got chills. *I know why they call him a legend,* she thought. *He doesn't understand it because he's up there, not out here watching.*

Emily was even entertained by the performers whose music she usually turned off when it came on the radio. She didn't mind the whine of the pedal steel guitar when she could watch the round-faced man who played it with such a tender touch.

It's the vigor of the live performances here that sets Branson apart. For audience and entertainers alike, the fountain of youth is right onstage, Emily jotted in her notebook. She'd use that in the story she would write next week.

Unlike award shows for actors, whose off-the-cuff performances sometimes failed to match the grace of their scripted roles, these entertainers were used to ad-libs in front of an audience. The show went off without a hitch, and Emily realized her earlier nervousness and apprehensions on the stars' behalf had been unfounded.

After two standing ovations and an encore, the curtain came down, and people began to stream out of the auditorium. With relief, Emily saw the Hacketts and the blonde heading up the opposite aisle. She hadn't seen Simmons in the audience.

Several people were heading backstage, so Emily joined the group and filed through the hallway. The electricity backstage was generated by the high level of energy coming from a happy bunch of entertainers. People were hugging each other, laughing, exchanging pats on the back, and proudly displaying their trophies. Lyle was surrounded by a group of enthusiastic admirers, so Emily hung in the background. Then Lyle saw her and called to her. He gave her a great bear hug.

"What'd you think?" he asked expectantly.

"I loved every minute of it," she said. "But most of all you."

Lyle laughed and released her from the hug. "Ah, you're a sweet lady, Miss Emily. I'm going to miss you, and I sure hope you'll come back and see us again sometime. Will you, darlin'?"

"I'll be back, Lyle," Emily said, and felt for that moment that it surely was true. "I've got a good friend now in Branson." Then other fans came over and Lyle was passing out the bear hugs.

Emily headed down the hall toward Glen Campbell's dressing room. It was crowded with fans, too. Emily worked her way through the crowd up to the tall, slim man and introduced herself.

"I tried to catch you before the show, but I ran out of time. Could you spare me a few minutes now?" she asked.

"Oh, yeah, you're that friend of Lyle's from Florida, aren't you?" Campbell said. "Just give me a chance to talk to some of these folks and change my clothes and I'll be right with you."

But it was nearly forty minutes later by the time the dressing room cleared of most of the well-wishers and another fifteen minutes before Campbell emerged wearing jeans and a golf shirt. While she waited, Emily had wandered around backstage. She had seen Monica talking animatedly to small groups of fans, but had not gone over to her. She couldn't offer her condolences when she wasn't supposed to know about Monica's secret with Stella. Nor did she want to risk the subject of Robert Simmons. It was best to keep some secrets. She didn't see Lyle anymore either, and assumed he had left the building.

Workers were already beginning to disassemble the set. With the house lights on, the sparkling silver stars hanging on wires from the backdrop had once again become mere painted plywood. For a moment, Emily felt sad and as empty as the stage. Her trip to Branson was leaving her with a tangled mix of emotions, things she'd have to think about a while. She thought of Jim. There were a lot of things she had to sort out when she got home.

There were few people left in the theater when Emily finally got to interview Glen Campbell. He was polite, but reserved and serious, not the cutup he'd seemed onstage. He looked as if he were well into the after-show letdown most performers experienced. And she was getting tired too, and thought about the hour's drive ahead of her, and the hassle of finding a place to stay, so she cut the interview short and didn't ask many of the questions she had planned. He seemed grateful it hadn't taken long and thanked her, shook her hand, then returned to his dressing room.

It was so quiet backstage now. And dark. Emily suddenly felt nervous as she headed for the back entrance. No one guarded the door and it clanged shut behind her. Outside, the sky had clouded over. She couldn't see any stars. A couple of pickup trucks and a black Chrysler remained parked behind the theater, and way across the parking lot, Emily saw her lone car.

No parking-lot attendants were around. Dotted throughout the parking lot, the clumps of shrubbery required by city landscape codes were the only sentinels. There was nothing out here to be scared of, she told herself, but the sound of her heels clacking against the pavement seemed to echo back from every hillside. Emily clutched her purse tightly and made a fist around her key chain as she'd learned in self-defense class. As she approached each clump of shrubbery, she slowed and squinted at the dark mass, looking for any sign of human movement. She thought of her pistol in the glove compartment and berated herself for not slipping it into her bag. With a clang, the stage door shut again. Emily jumped and looked back to see Campbell get into a pickup and drive away in the opposite direction.

I should have asked him for a ride to my car, Emily thought, stepping up her pace. Don't be such a goose.

As she neared her car, she focused on the ground beneath the car and saw no figure lurking there, waiting to grab her ankles. She stood still for a moment and watched the bushes near her car. Nothing moved. She walked up to the car and slid the key into the lock as she checked the backseat.

The smell of English Leather and cigarettes filled her nostrils at the same time she saw his reflection in the car window. John Hackett was on her, grabbing her from behind. He spun her around and slammed her against the car. Her head went backward, hitting the car roof with a bang. Hackett had one hand around her throat, and she could see a gun gleaming in his other hand, pointed at her face.

"I thought we'd have a little going-away party for you," Hackett said. "Don't scream or do anything stupid or I'll end the party right here."

He pressed the pistol hard against her cheek. Still holding her by the throat, Hackett jerked Emily forward, then slammed her against the car again. He poked the pistol into her side and kissed her on the mouth. Emily looked into the black hole of his pupil so close to her face and tried to turn her head, but he clutched her throat tighter.

"That's just a little kiss for starters, baby," he said. "You'll soon find out what all the ladies like so much about ol' John. I wouldn't want you going off thinking Stella was right about me."

For a moment Emily couldn't think what he was talking about. She could barely breathe. Hackett's body was against her, pinning her to the car.

"I know you heard what Stella was saying to me, you eavesdropping little bitch. Did you think I could let you get away after that? Stella was wrong, you know. She was lying, trying to make me feel bad. There are plenty of women in town who would testify to my manhood. Plenty. And you're about to join the club. You know I didn't mean to push Stella off the balcony," Hackett rasped. "I just wanted to shake some sense into her, make her stop lying. You understand that, don't you?" He shook her.

Emily nodded as much as she could. Hackett was breathing heavily. "You understand I couldn't let her go around telling people that I couldn't perform anymore, don't you? A thing like that can hurt a person. And it wasn't true. You'll see."

He kissed Emily's cheek. "I did her a favor, you know? She was young and perfect. Did you see her lying there? She looked beautiful. That's how people will remember her. She'll always be twenty-three. And she'll always be mine. I did Stella a lot of favors."

Hackett loosened his grip on Emily's throat. "Now I'm going to let go of your throat, but if you scream, I'll shoot you. No one's around to hear you anyway. I want you to get in the car and slide across the seat. Then we're going for a ride out to where you'll take a wrong turn off a big hill. So don't do anything stupid. I tried to warn you, you know. I watched you until you found my spy hole. I read your list of suspects. You're a regular Sherlock Holmes." Hackett tried to laugh, but it turned into a retching cough right in Emily's face.

"I warned you to get out of town, and I even took care of your furry little friend," he said, gasping. "But you're not a smart lady. Not smart at all. Instead of taking my kind advice and getting out of here, you told the sheriff tonight you wanted to talk to him tomorrow. Well, baby, there ain't no tomorrow for you. By the time anyone thinks to go looking for you, you won't have any stories to tell."

Hackett grabbed her arm, pulled her around, and

pushed her forward against the car. Emily felt her necklace break and heard the crystals hit the ground and scatter.

Her keys were still in the lock, and he unlocked the door and opened it. He grabbed her by the back of her neck, and she felt the gun's muzzle against her spine.

"Now get in and slide over," Hackett said. "Don't try anything or you won't live long enough for the big treat I've got for you."

Emily ducked down to get into the car. She put her right hand on the seat and held the steering wheel in her left hand as she slid across. She tried to remember exactly how the glove compartment opened as she slid under the steering wheel, tried to think of how the gun lay. She was halfway across the seat, between the glove compartment and Hackett.

"Could I have a cigarette?" Emily asked. Her voice was husky from Hackett's choking grip.

"Yeah, yeah, just get in," Hackett said. Holding the pistol in his right hand, he reached into his jacket's breast pocket and took out the pack. He shook one out and put it in his mouth. He laid the pack on top of the car and reached into his pocket again. Emily watched him over her shoulder. Now both her hands were on the dashboard, above the glove compartment. Hackett pulled out a cigarette lighter. Emily watched him put it to the cigarette. He lit the lighter and Emily saw the flame reflected in his jagged eye as his gaze shifted from her for a moment to glance at the flame.

Emily moved. The glove compartment door opened easily, the gun was in her hand and she turned, firing all in one smooth motion. The force of the shot propelled Hackett backward. His gun went off as he hit the pavement. Emily sat motionless while the silence came back. Hackett didn't move. Then she saw someone running toward the car and aimed again.

"Emily! Don't shoot!" Just in time, she recognized Lyle and brought the muzzle up. Then Lyle was leaning in. "You all right? You all right?"

Emily nodded. Her ears were ringing, and her head and throat throbbed. "Sit still," he said, squatting down to take the gun from Hackett's hand.

Lyle stood up and Emily could see he was holding a baseball bat. John Hackett lay on his back. His eyes were open and the front of his shirt was dark with blood. In the distance, Emily heard a siren's wail.

While she continued to stare at Hackett, Lyle came around the car. "Unlock this door." She put the pistol on the dashboard and pulled up the button. Lyle took her hand and helped her out of the car. Emily's knees were weak, but Lyle held her tightly.

"I'm sorry," he said. "I'm so sorry I didn't stop him sooner. Come sit down over here." Lyle led her to the curb and pulled the silver flask out of his pocket. "Have a sip of this, darlin'," he said. "It'll calm you down."

The Southern Comfort tasted sweet, and the hot jolt of it brought back her breath and calmed her racing pulse a little. She handed it back to Lyle.

"Thank you," she said hoarsely. "Is he dead?"

"Yes. You saved me the trouble of putting a dent in his head with my Louisville Slugger. I saw him heading for your car when I came out to go home, and I watched him hide himself in the bushes. I grabbed my bat and came around the other side of the parking lot and worked my way over to that next planter and watched for you to come out. I should have been smart and come back in and gotten you and stayed with you until you were safely away, but I figured he'd want to brag to you about killing Stella, and

I wanted to hear it. I wasn't sure until now that he did it. I didn't know he had a gun, or I would never have let you get into such a dangerous situation. I'm sorry, Emily. You could have been killed, and I was just thinking about how good it would feel to testify to what I heard and watch them lock him up." Lyle put his arm around Emily. "You'll never be back to the Ozarks after all this, will you, baby?"

"I don't know. What will happen to that video tape he had of you?"

"That doesn't matter anymore. I looked out at that audience tonight and said to myself, 'Lyle, that's your family. They're the only family you're ever going to have.' If the tape comes out, I'm going to have to trust them. I just hope they love me enough to forgive an old man's mistake. If not, I'll have to take my punishment just like he did."

The sounds of sirens neared. Lyle pulled out his pocket phone. "This finally turned out to be good for something."

"I killed him," Emily whispered.

"You defended yourself. Thank God you were prepared and had the presence of mind to do it. You ought to get a medal for your community service."

Sheriff Turner listened silently to Lyle's account. "I need you both to ride downtown and make a statement. We'll have the deputy bring your car, and we'll find you a place to stay tonight, Miss Stone. You're in no condition for a long drive." Lyle and Emily rode in the back of the sheriff's car. As they left the parking lot, an ambulance arrived. No one said a word and Lyle kept his arm around Emily's shoulders.

By the time Emily had finished telling Turner the whole story, including what she'd overheard upstairs in the mansion, it was nearly three A.M.

196

"I wish you would have told me all this to begin with," Turner said.

"So do I. But would you have arrested him based on what I overheard?"

"No. But it might have been the pressure I needed to get Irene to stop protecting him. I half thought she might have been the one who pushed Stella."

When the sheriff was through with Emily, she went out to the waiting room where Lyle slumped on a couch. Dark circles under his eyes defined his fatigue. He held Emily for a moment, but it couldn't have been called a bear hug.

"Goodbye, Emily." He held her hand in both of his. "I hope we'll meet again."

"I'm sure we will, Lyle." She thought, as she watched him walk away, that despite how tired the man must have been, his shoulders were a little straighter than she'd ever seen them.

A deputy drove Emily to a small motel, an old place, too rundown to attract many tourists. The sheriff's department leased a couple of rooms there that they could use to lodge abused women after family disputes. Her rental car was parked outside, and the deputy carried her bags into the room and asked if there was anything he could get for her.

She thought for a moment of asking him if he had a cigarette, but then she remembered the smell of John Hackett. She felt her stomach contract, felt the vomit rise in her throat. She shook her head and waved the deputy out the door just in time to make it to the toilet.

When the sickness was over, Emily ran cold water on a washcloth and wiped her face. She looked in the mirror and then turned and flopped facedown on the bed and sobbed. As the tensions ebbed out of her, she felt the wet spot under her cheek and thought of the countless lonely,

bruised women who must have cried into that green che-
nille bedspread.

After a while, the tears ran out, and she rolled over on
her back on the soft lumpy mattress. Outside, the red and
green neon sign flashed on and off, on and off. "Vacancy
. . . Vacancy . . . Vacancy."

Emily blew her nose and picked up the phone and
dialed. "Hello. It's Emily. I know it's late, but I just wanted
to hear your voice. No, I'm all right. Really, I'm all right
now." She wiped her nose. "I'll tell you all about it tomorrow night when I get home. My plane gets in at eight-fif-
teen. Do you think you could pick me up? Thanks, Jim. I
missed you, too." She ran her fingers through her hair.
"Jim, maybe sometime we can plan a trip back here. And
we'll bring Mother, too. I found a place I want to take you
both for Sunday dinner."

Appendix ✠

Porphyria's Lover

by Robert Browning

The rain set early in to-night,
    The sullen wind was soon awake,
It tore the elm-tops down for spite,
    And did its worst to vex the lake:
    I listened with heart fit to break.
When glided in Porphyria; straight
    She shut the cold out and the storm,
And kneeled and made the cheerless grate
    Blaze up, and all the cottage warm;
    Which done, she rose, and from her form
Withdrew the dripping cloak and shawl,
    And laid her soiled gloves by, untied
Her hat and let the damp hair fall,
    And, last, she sat down by my side
    And called me. When no voice replied,
She put my arm about her waist,
    And made her smooth white shoulder bare
And all her yellow hair displaced,
    And, stooping, made my cheek lie there,
    And spread, o'er all, her yellow hair,
Murmuring how she loved me—she
    Too weak, for all her heart's endeavour,
To set its struggling passion free
    From pride, and vainer ties dissever,
    And give herself to me forever.

But passion sometimes would prevail,
        Nor could to-night's gay feast restrain
A sudden thought of one so pale
        For love of her, and all in vain:
        So, she was come through wind and rain
Be sure I looked up at her eyes
        Happy and proud; at last I knew
Porphyria worshipped me; surprise
        Made my heart swell, and still it grew
        While I debated what to do.
That moment she was mine, mine, fair,
        Perfectly pure and good: I found
A thing to do, and all her hair
        In one long yellow string I wound
        Three times her little throat around,
And strangled her. No pain felt she;
        I am quite sure she felt no pain.
As a shut bud that holds a bee,
        I warily oped her lids: again
        Laughed the blue eyes without a stain.
And I untightened next the tress
        About her neck; her cheek once more
Blushed bright beneath my burning kiss:
        I propped her head up as before,
        Only, this time my shoulder bore
Her head, which droops upon it still:
        The smiling rosy little head,
So glad it has its utmost will,
        That all it scorned at once is fled,
        And I, its love, am gained instead!
Porphyria's love: she guessed not how
        Her darling one wish would be heard.
And thus we sit together now,
        And all night long we have not stirred,
        And yet God has not said a word!